"The Trouble With You, Riggs, Is That You're Always Just Kidding,"

Kathleen said. "You never take anything seriously."

"Meaning what?" Mel asked.

"Meaning you're so good at laughing things off, you couldn't even acknowledge it when things started going wrong between us," she answered in a low voice.

"I knew it. I just didn't want to admit it," he said quietly. "If anybody had reason to be unhappy, it was me."

She stared incredulously. "You?"

He was serious now, no doubt about that. "I was the one who had to compete with my own wife while I was getting my career off the ground."

"Your career? What about—" Kathleen stopped short. "You don't understand now any more than you did then." She stood up. "I'd like to say it's been fun, but I think you know better."

Mel watched her leave, and he wondered why, after all these years, it still hurt so much.

Dear Reader,

Happy 1992, and welcome to Silhouette Desire! For those of you who are new readers, I must say I think you're starting the year off right—with wonderful romance. If you're a regular Desire fan, you already know what delicious stories are in store for you... this month *and* this year. I wish I could tell you the exciting things planned for you in 1992, but that would be giving all of my secrets away. But I will admit that it's going to be a great year.

As for January, what better way to kick off a new year of *Man of the Month* stories than with a sensuous, satisfying love story from Ann Major, *A Knight in Tarnished Armor.* And don't miss any of 1992's *Man of the Month* books, including stories written by Diana Palmer, Annette Broadrick, Dixie Browning, Sherryl Woods and Laura Leone—and that's just half of my lineup!

This month is completed with books by Barbara Boswell, Beverly Barton, Cathryn Clare, Jean Barrett and Toni Collins. They're all terrific; don't miss a single one.

And remember, don't hesitate to write and tell me what you think of the books. I'm always glad to receive reader feedback.

So go wild with Desire... until next month,

Lucia Macro
Senior Editor

TONI COLLINS

IMMORAL SUPPORT

SILHOUETTE *Desire*®

Published by Silhouette Books New York

America's Publisher of Contemporary Romance

SILHOUETTE BOOKS
300 East 42nd St., New York, N.Y. 10017

IMMORAL SUPPORT

ISBN: 0-373-05686-9

First Silhouette Books printing January 1992

Printed in the U.S.A.

Books by Toni Collins

Silhouette Desire
Immoral Support #686

Silhouette Romance
Ms. Maxwell and Son #664

TONI COLLINS

is a bestselling author of mainstream novels under her real name. She has worked in numerous occupations, all with one goal in mind: to one day realize her dream of being a full-time writer.

When Ms. Collins began writing for Silhouette Books, she felt a greater freedom with the category romance format, since she felt that she "could do things in this book that simply didn't fit" her mainstream books.

Ms. Collins has traveled extensively and now lives in St. Louis with her husband and son.

Dedicated to the unsung heroes of the St. Louis press, none of whom made it into the pages of this book but were an inspiration just the same.

One
___

"**W**e've really got to stop meeting like this."

"For once, we agree on something," Kathleen Wilder acknowledged with mild annoyance as Mel Riggs squeezed into the crowded elevator behind her and flashed her a grin worthy of a toothpaste ad. Damn him, anyway, she thought irritably as she managed, but not without some difficulty, to tuck her slim reporter's notebook into her oversize black leather shoulder bag. She raised her hand, secretly wanting to slap that smug expression off his face, but settled for raking it through her long, honey-blond curls instead. He enjoyed this. He enjoyed driving her up the wall. At every available opportunity he reminded her that he worked for the city's number one daily newspaper while she'd spent the past five years as a reporter for a considerably smaller suburban paper. Theirs was a rivalry, however, that actually went back much further than that, to a time when the two of them were just out of college, working for a small newspaper in a small town in southwestern Michigan—and newlyweds.

Their colleagues at their respective papers found it hard to believe that they'd ever been husband and wife. There were times Kathleen found it hard to believe herself. They'd been married for two years, divorced ten. And now at thirty-three, she was still struggling to make a name for herself here while he was the closest thing Saint Louis had to a real live "celebrity journalist"—and he thoroughly enjoyed reminding her of it.

But most of all, he enjoyed beating her out on a story—which he almost always did.

"Y'know, Wilder," he was saying, "if I didn't know better, I'd think you didn't like me or something."

She looked at him. He was still smiling, the jerk. He was, she had to admit—if only to herself—a good-looking jerk. He wasn't all that tall, maybe a couple of inches taller than she was, at the most.

He'd always hated it when she wore heels because she would be taller than he was. Maybe that was why she wore them so often these days. His features were strong, his eyes a light blue-gray that reminded her of a stormy ocean. His dark brown hair—Hershey's brown, she called it on good days (she had another name for it on bad days)—was quite unruly and long enough to cover the collar of his leather bomber jacket. He wore a Detroit Tigers T-shirt, jeans and sneakers, and looked more like an undercover narc than a thirty-five-year-old, Pulitzer Prize-winning journalist. Yeah...the jerk was good-looking, all right. Trouble was, he knew it. He'd always known it.

"If you didn't know better..." Kathleen repeated slowly, carefully, suppressing a smile. "For once, Riggs, your sources have failed you."

Before he could respond—and she was certain he would have, he always did—the elevator came to a stop at the ground floor with a slight jerking motion. Kathleen was the first to exit, heading across the busy lobby of the Saint Louis County Courthouse at a surprisingly fast clip, given the fact that she was wearing three-inch heels, not looking back as she made her way to the revolving doors leading to South Central Avenue.

She wasn't sure exactly what it was about Riggs that bugged her most—his looks since, having been married to him, she automatically distrusted any man who looked that good; his cocky self-assurance, which drove her up the wall; or his incredible success (she thought it incredible, anyway), which she wasn't at all sure he deserved. He was a good reporter, yes, but was he *that* good? Good enough to have won a Pulitzer? Good enough to be making the kind of money few journalists in this part of the country were paid?

Yeah, maybe he *was* that good, much as she hated to admit it.

She and Riggs definitely went back a long way. She remembered well—perhaps too well—the first time their paths had crossed. She'd just started at the paper in Paw Paw as a general assignment reporter and had been sent to cover a story in a suburban community with which she didn't even have a passing familiarity. She'd stopped at a gas station to ask directions. The only attendant on duty that day had been busy with a customer, so she'd approached the man who was fighting a losing battle with a contrary soda-vending machine just inside the grimy garage. No, he didn't work there, he'd told her, but he did know the area quite well and would be more than happy to direct a reporter to her story.

Following his directions, it had taken her over an hour to reach her destination—and even longer to find her way back to the newspaper office. By the time she got back and filed her story, it was too late to make the next edition. That was when she learned the identity of the man at the gas station: Melvin Riggs.

He'd thought it was funny—but she'd been furious with him, so to atone for the error of his ways, he'd talked her into letting him take her out to dinner. Kathleen had been amazed at how much she'd enjoyed herself, considering how little they had in common, so when he asked her out again, she'd accepted without hesitation.

Theirs had been a whirlwind courtship—in the most literal sense of the word. It had been wild and zany and tempestuous and passionate, and she'd been more in love with him than she'd ever dreamed possible. But she'd known even then that the differences in their personalities would present problems. She remembered the night he proposed like it was yesterday....

"Why don't we get married?" he had suggested casually.

She laughed aloud, thinking he was joking. "Is that supposed to be a proposal?" she wanted to know.

He wasn't smiling. "It's the only one you're going to get."

Kathleen stared at him for a moment. "You're serious!" she gasped.

"You act like you're surprised or something."

"Well—I am!"

"I don't see why."

"We haven't been seeing each other all that long."

"Long enough."

"Three months."

"Three months, two weeks and five days," he corrected her.

She was touched that he'd remembered. But then, Mel had a memory like a computer. "You do realize we're about as different as two people can be," she pointed out.

He grinned. "I'd have to be dead not to know it."

"We'd have about as much chance of making it work as the Berlin Wall has of coming down in our lifetime."

"Less," he said. "But then, I never could resist a challenge."

Logic told her—even that night—that they didn't have a snowball's chance in you-know-where of making a go of it. But while her head was saying no, her heart was screaming yes, yes, yes....

I should've listened to my head, she now thought ruefully, unlocking her car door.

"Hello again!"

She looked up. There he was, coming toward her. "Don't you have a home to go to, Riggs?" she asked irritably.

"Sure I do. That's where I'm headed now."

She watched him walk right on by, headed for his own car, which was parked on the other side of the lot. Why did she have to come here, anyway? Why did she have to end up in the same city where her ex-husband had taken up residence?

And why did he still get to her?

Ms. Kathleen Wilder was really some piece of work.

Mel had known that the first time he saw her. She was a real class act, with her long, blond hair and smoky eyes. She was tall and dressed a lot better these days than he figured she could afford on what she had to be making at the *Daily Mirror*. After all, it wasn't part of the Newspaper Guild, which meant the *Daily Mirror* people weren't making nearly as much as *Star* reporters. But Kathy Wilder was definitely a class act, no matter how she was doing it. She had a husky voice for a woman, which he found unexpectedly sexy. That was the first thing that attracted him to her. One of the first things, anyway. Too bad it hadn't worked out, he thought now. The chemistry between them had been incredible. A lot of women had passed through his life since the divorce, but there had never been anybody like her—not before and not since.

Trouble was, they'd never be able to live under the same roof again. They were having trouble now, living in the same city!

He signaled the bartender for another beer. No point in dwelling on it. She hated his guts. Not that that was unusual when it came to his relationships with women—starting with his mother, who'd walked out on his father, leaving him and her seven-year-old son behind when she decided one day to go off and "pursue her dreams." He'd never told Kathy about that. He'd never told anyone. It was one of those things he'd never been able to discuss. Too painful.

He looked up as Kathleen came into the bar. She smiled when she saw him. "I see you still celebrate payday the same way," she commented, eyeing his drink.

"I thought I was safe here," he droned. "You always hated this kind of place."

"I still do," she assured him. "I'm just meeting someone here."

"I see," he said with a nod.

She looked at her watch. "I'm early," she said, more to herself than to him. "I didn't have time to go home, so..."

"You don't have to explain it to me."

"I know that," she responded coldly.

He hesitated for a moment. "Sit down. I'll buy you a drink."

She shook her head. "No, thanks."

He picked up his drink and took a long swallow. "I know what you think of the guys who hang out in bars. Nobody will come near you if you're sitting here with me."

She met his gaze. "That's for sure."

"If you're worried about your date, don't," he said. "Nobody in town who recognizes either of us would ever think there could be anything going on between us."

She laughed at the thought. "You've got that right."

"C'mon," he persisted. "Let me buy you a drink."

"What have you got in mind?" she asked suspiciously. "Hemlock?"

"I didn't think that would work on you."

"That's it." She started to walk away, but he grabbed her hand.

"Loosen up, Kathy," he said in a voice barely above a whisper. "I was just kidding."

"You're always 'just kidding,' Riggs," she hissed. "That's the trouble with you, you know. You almost never take anything seriously."

"Wrong. I take a lot of things seriously."

"Always the wrong things," she said, seating herself on the stool next to him.

"Meaning what?"

"Meaning you're so good at laughing things off, you couldn't even acknowledge it when things started going wrong between us," she said in a low voice.

"I knew it. I just didn't want to admit it," he said quietly. "It was kind of hard to deny the marriage was over when I came home that day and found everything I owned in cardboard boxes on the front porch. I only beat the Goodwill truck by ten minutes."

"I didn't call Goodwill." She tried not to laugh.

"Yeah, right." He rolled his eyes skyward. "They just happened to be in the neighborhood, right?"

"I couldn't make you open up. I couldn't get you to tell me what was wrong," she recalled. "I just couldn't take it anymore, Mel. I had to get drastic."

"Calling Goodwill was definitely drastic." He finished his drink and signaled the bartender for a refill.

"See?" The frustration level in her voice raised several decibels. "Even now, you're making jokes. You never deal with a problem, you never talk about it, you just avoid it."

"I didn't have to deal with that one." He wasn't smiling now. "You dealt with it for both of us by booting me out."

"You left me no choice."

He turned to face her. "You know, if anybody had a reason to be unhappy, it was me," he told her.

She stared incredulously. *"You?"*

"Yeah, me." He was serious now, no doubt about that. "I was the one who had to compete with my own wife while I was getting my career off the ground."

"*Your* career? What about—" She stopped short, seeing her date come through the door. "What's the use? You wouldn't understand now any more than you did then." She stood up. "Thanks for the drink. I'd like to say it's been fun, but I think you know better."

He watched her leave, and he wondered why, after all these years, it still hurt so much.

"You're still here?" Kathleen asked, surprised to see her editor in the newsroom when she returned late that evening to write and file the story she'd been working on. "Has war been declared?"

Gerry Hancock looked up from the copy he'd been reading. When Gerry worked late, which he often did, he always looked like he had a monumental hangover. He was forty-seven and looked a good fifteen years older. Occupational hazard, he called it.

"No war," he assured her, shaking his head. "Just some Russian diplomat who croaked at a real inconvenient time."

"And you've got to do the story," Kathleen guessed, putting her bag down on the desk.

"Almost as bad," Gerry said with a nod. "I had to come up with a headline. How's this?"

She took the yellow legal pad he handed her. Everything he'd scribbled on it had been scratched out except for five words, printed in block letters: DEAD RED FOUND IN BED

She laughed aloud. "Are you really going to print this?"

He grinned, taking it back. "No, but it's late, and if I don't laugh, I'll probably cry."

"Getting a little punchy, are we?"

"I don't know about 'we,' but I could use a ten-year sabbatical," he said with an exaggerated groan. "What about you, kiddo? Why are you here?"

"Got a story to file—and I want another look at the Rollins file." She took off her jacket and hung it on the back of the chair.

"Spending a lot of time on that one, aren't you?" Gerry observed.

"I'm writing a book on it."

"Yeah? Got a contract?"

"Not yet, but I think I will very soon now," she said confidently. "Remember Darcy McDonough?"

He nodded. "That novelist you interviewed a while back."

"Well, she sent me to her agent, Carla Phillips, in New York," Kathleen explained. "Now Carla's representing me, too—and very optimistic about the project."

Gerry let out a low whistle. "I'm impressed. I've heard good things about her. She's got a lot of heavy hitters on her roster."

"So I've heard." Kathleen sat down at her desk and switched on the computer terminal. "Wish me luck, Gerry."

"Only if you promise not to quit."

It was past midnight when Kathleen finally left the *Daily Mirror* building. Driving home to her small apartment in the Central West End, she thought about the direction her life was taking. She'd always set her goals, then reassessed them every five years. She'd been at the paper five years last month, so she was now a little behind in rethinking the goals of five years ago. She supposed it was because she'd been happy at the paper, right from the start. She liked the job, she liked the people, and she'd enjoyed most of the interviews, especially since she'd moved to features last year. She liked doing features—it allowed for more creativity than news reporting. It had also allowed her to steer clear of Riggs—until now.

She'd known when she asked her editor to put her on the Rollins case that she'd be crossing Mel's path more than once before it was over. It was his kind of story—a well-known socialite accused of killing his wife. The prosecution was basing its case solely on circumstantial evidence, but the public outrage was so fierce that everyone—literally everyone—was sure he was guilty as sin. Yes, a case like this one was meant for the Melvin Riggs by-line—and she'd known he'd be like a vulture circling the courthouse, waiting for the verdict.

That, after all, was what made him such a good crime reporter. That was what had won him the Pulitzer. It was also what had ruined their marriage, in a way.

She thought about what he'd said in the bar. He actually saw himself as the injured party! He really couldn't stand the idea of having to compete—as he saw it—with his own wife. I'm as bad as he is, she thought. All of the signs were there, but I didn't see them. Not then, anyway.

She remembered now how he'd made jokes—at least she'd thought they were jokes at the time—about the competition between them, sarcastic remarks about his wife keeping him on his toes at the paper because she was out to get his job. Things like that, that seemed so innocent at the time. With Mel it had never been easy to tell if he was joking or not.

Apparently that was one time he hadn't been.

In all the time they'd been together, which hadn't been all that long but long enough, she'd never realized how much it had bothered him. But then, he'd known she was a reporter when he married her—an inexperienced reporter, but still a reporter. She hadn't misled him—he knew how important her work was to her.

Or did he?

Why did it bother him so much? She still didn't know. She supposed it was male ego, but that didn't even make sense because she'd never been any real competition for him, even back then. Their bosses had considered her a good writer, a fair reporter—with promise—but it was Mel who'd been the star player on the team, right from the beginning.

She'd had to work twice as hard as anybody else just to keep up with him. She'd thought if she could make him proud of her, he'd change his mind. She'd thought wrong. The last thing he wanted was for her to be a success. The more she accomplished, the more the tension between them increased, until finally she could no longer avoid reality.

Their marriage could not be saved.

Maybe I'm just not cut out for marriage, she thought now. Maybe Helen Gurley Brown can "have it all," but not me. Maybe I'm just meant to be a career woman. Period.

Maybe that was what had made her decide to write the book. Oh, she'd wanted to write a book for a long time—but until she'd actually started this book, she'd always assumed she'd write novels. Her interest had always leaned toward fiction. The book she was writing, until the day she'd decided to write it, was the last thing she'd ever considered doing. Yet here she was, not only writing it, but contemplating what she would do if forced to choose between her job and the book. It certainly wouldn't be an easy choice to make.

When she got home, she found a message from her agent on the answering machine. "Kathleen, it's Carla. I need to talk to you right away."

No explanation, nothing. Kathleen didn't have to look at the clock to know it was too late to call tonight. And it was an hour later in New York.

Kathleen frowned. It was going to be a long night.

She called her agent first thing the next morning. "Thanks for costing me a night's sleep," she grumbled. "What's up?"

"Good news," Carla responded. "You have a contract. Your book has been sold."

TWO

Kathleen thought about it as she drove to work. She'd done it. She had a contract. She was going to write a book. She was going to write a book that would be *published*. She couldn't believe it—and she was sure no one else would, either. Mel certainly wouldn't.

Mel.

She couldn't wait to tell him. He'd always done his best to discourage her, to undermine her self-confidence on a professional level. He'd never wanted her to succeed.

Well, Melvin, I made it in spite of you, she thought, pleased with herself. And I'm going to rub your nose in it.

"It's the hot line!"

Mel looked up from the computer terminal at his desk. "Yeah? Who is it?"

"She didn't give her name—but then, the ones who call for you never do."

He got to his feet and made his way through the maze of cubicles that served as reporters' offices. At the back of the newsroom, on a table by itself, was a very old, red, rotary-type phone. The dial had been removed a long time ago so that the phone could only be used for incoming calls.

Mel shot the reporter holding the receiver a baleful glance as he snatched it and put it to his ear. "Riggs," he identified himself.

"Hi there, Riggs. Wilder here."

"Kathy?"

"The one and only."

"Why are you calling on this line—"

"I've got a hot news tip for you, Riggs," she said, feigning urgency in her voice.

"Yeah, right."

"Oh, I'm serious," she assured him. "This is big news, Melvin, real big news. I now have a contract to write a book on the Rollins case."

"You're kidding!"

"Am I laughing?"

"How'd you get a contract? Who—"

"Pelham and Parker—and they were looking for someone to do a book on it, believe it or not."

"But why you?"

"Why not me?" she shot back, sounding more than a little insulted.

"No—I mean, how did they find you?"

"My agent. She called me to their attention."

"Since when do you have an agent?"

She laughed, obviously enjoying this. "Since I decided I wanted to write a book," she said. "Listen, Melvin, I've got to run. I'd really love to chat, but I'm holding down two jobs now. I just wanted you to be the first to know."

The receiver clicked in his ear. He hung up slowly. A book contract? Kathy? He still couldn't figure how that could have happened. She wasn't exactly a household word. Her stuff wasn't nationally syndicated or anything like that. She'd always just missed the boat when the journalism awards were handed out. And she worked for a relatively small paper.

So how had she managed to get herself a book contract?

* * *

Across town Kathleen sat at her desk in the middle of the newsroom, a look of deep satisfaction on her face. She'd been able to hear the envy in his voice, and she'd loved every minute of it. For once, she'd managed to top him at something.

"If you don't look like the cat that swallowed the canary."

She looked up. Hal Waggoner, the reporter who occupied the desk across from hers, was grinning as though he'd just read her mind. "Don't let the boss hear you saying things like that," she warned. "Using clichés is grounds for dismissal, you know."

"Yeah, right. So what's up?"

"Well, if you must know, I've finally managed to beat Melvin Riggs at something."

He laughed. "And just what would that be?"

Kathleen hesitated momentarily. He'd laughed because he thought it wasn't possible that she could top Riggs at anything. No one thought it possible. Not even her own colleagues at her own paper.

"You'll find out soon enough," she told him.

She'd show him. She'd show all of them.

"Who'd have thought it?"

Though he said it aloud, he'd been asking the question more of himself than anyone else in the office. Richard Head, the *Star*'s most widely syndicated columnist, who had been standing within earshot, responded. "Thought what?"

Mel's head jerked up. He looked at Richard for a moment, not realizing at first that anyone could have heard him. Richard was a friend, but heck, he was a slob—rumpled, always in need of a shave, walked with a slow, lazy shuffle, wore an old, tattered raincoat. And unspeakably gaudy ties.

"Huh?"

"You just said, and I quote, 'Who'd have thought it?' end quote," said Richard. "I repeat—who'd have thought what?"

Mel shook his head. "Kathy—would you believe she just got a contract to do a book on the Rollins case?"

Richard grinned, pouring himself a cup of coffee. "After fifteen years in this business, I'd believe just about anything." He paused. "Anyway, why should it bother you that your ex has got a book deal?"

"It doesn't. I'm just amazed, that's all." He ran a hand through his hair, frustrated. "I mean, if they want somebody to write a book, seems to me they'd want somebody who was better known—"

"Like you?" Richard asked with a knowing smile.

"Well—yeah!"

"Sour grapes?"

"Are you kidding?"

"Come on, Mel—you two have been in competition with each other for the past five years," Richard reminded him—as if he'd needed to be reminded. "Ever since she started at the *Daily Mirror,* you two have spent all of your time trying to beat each other to stories as if this was some kind of journalistic Olympics and you're both going for the gold."

"You should be writing fiction, Rich," he chuckled. "You have one vivid imagination."

"Okay. Deny it if you want—but everybody knows it."

Mel waved him off. "Go rain on somebody else's parade, will you?"

The truth, he decided, definitely hurt.

The next time he saw her was, appropriately, at the courthouse.

She was standing outside the courtroom with a couple of TV reporters, waiting to be allowed to go inside. He'd intended to ignore her, to walk right past her and act as if he hadn't seen her, but she made sure that wasn't possible.

"Hi, Riggs," she called out to him.

He couldn't pretend not to hear her. Everyone within earshot had heard her. He looked her way and forced a smile. "Hi there, Wilder," he responded with a faked cheerfulness.

She was enjoying this. He'd never thought of her as malicious, but there was no doubt about it. She was enjoying this.

"She's rubbing my nose in it," he told Richard over lunch at Maggie O'Brien's, an Irish pub and restaurant on Market Street downtown.

"Ex-wives are like that, Riggs," Richard observed between bites. "Listen to the voice of experience here. Ex-wives were put on this earth to make men think they've died and gone south."

"Kathy's never been mean." Mel was surprised to find himself defending her. "She's just—ambitious." Which was just as bad in his book.

Richard shook his head. "I've been married five times—and every one of my divorces was like a reenactment of Custer's Last Stand," he maintained. "They're *all* mean, pal."

Mel smiled. Richard had five ex-wives while everyone still wondered how he'd even managed to talk *one* woman into marrying him. He was a nice enough guy, but hardly the type anyone would have thought of as a lady-killer. "If you're so down on women," Mel began, "why'd you get married so many times?"

Richard shrugged. "Call it optimism. I always figured, 'This one's different. This one's going to work.' But they never did."

"Well, a building doesn't have to fall on me," Mel said, putting down his fork. "Once is enough as far as I'm concerned."

He couldn't admit he'd never wanted anyone but Kathleen.

"I rubbed his nose in it." Across town Kathleen was having lunch with Darcy McDonough, a flamboyant redhead as notorious for her outrageousness as she was for the steamy novels she wrote. They were lunching at Amighetti's, a small bakery-restaurant in the predominantly Italian section of town known as The Hill.

Darcy grinned. "Sometimes I get the feeling that coming out on top of your ex-husband—if you'll pardon the expression—is more important to you than the book itself."

"Sometimes, I feel that way myself," Kathleen admitted. "I can't quite explain it, but I've always felt I had to prove myself to Mel—prove I was his equal. Does that make sense to you?"

"Not really," Darcy answered honestly.

"Mel didn't want me working at the paper after we got married. He was subtle about it at first, but I knew. What I didn't know was why," Kathleen recalled. "For a while, I thought maybe he was embarrassed, that he knew I was never quite in his league and figured everybody else at the paper knew it, too. But it turned out he didn't want to compete with me. Isn't that a laugh?"

"It always comes down to good old male ego, doesn't it?" Darcy stated more than asked.

"Be serious, Darcy."

"Sorry, but you're asking the wrong person for advice when it comes to matters of the heart," Darcy pointed out. "I had the dumb luck to fall for a guy who's on the road more than he's home." Darcy's husband, Patrick, was a tabloid reporter who did a great deal of traveling. "At the rate we're going, if I ever do get pregnant, we'll be looking for three guys on camels and a bright star in the East."

"One thing I can be grateful for—Mel and I at least had the good sense to take precautions," Kathleen said darkly.

"You don't want kids?"

"I don't want to raise them alone—which is what I'd be doing if Mel and I had had any."

She'd never admit that she'd always wondered what it would be like to have a little boy who looked just like his father.

"Why does it bother you so much?" Richard asked.

"Why does what bother me?" Mel asked testily.

"This book deal of Kathy's?"

"It doesn't bother me—"

"Come on, Mel—this is me you're talking to," Richard reminded him.

"You didn't let me finish," Mel snapped. "It's not the deal that bugs me. It's why she's doing it."

"Which is?"

"To get back at me, of course."

"You sure about that?"

"I know my ex-wife."

"He can't stand it that I've got this book deal," Kathleen told Darcy.

"And you're glad he can't," Darcy concluded.

"It doesn't matter to me one way or the other," Kathleen insisted.

"Sure it doesn't. This is me you're talking to, remember?"

"It doesn't!"

"Yeah, right."

"He thinks I'm doing this just to get to him, you know."

"What makes you so sure?"

"I know my ex-husband."

"You're still in love with her," Richard declared.

Mel laughed at the thought. "Don't be ridiculous!"

"What's ridiculous, pal, is that you've got it bad and can't admit it."

"You make me sound like an alcoholic," Mel chuckled.

"Close, Riggs. Real close."

"You're still in love with him," Darcy insisted.

Kathleen almost strangled on her drink. "Don't be ridiculous!"

"Deny it if you want," Darcy told her, "but you are still hung up on him."

"In your wildest dreams," Kathleen insisted.

"And you always called *me* a vulture!"

Kathleen heard Mel before she saw him. He was crossing the parking lot, coming toward her as she was getting out of her car. "Just doing my job," she said coolly.

He grinned. "Which one?"

"It really bugs you, doesn't it?"

"What?"

"That I'm doing the book."

He chuckled. "Don't flatter yourself, honey."

"Come on, Melvin—you never could stand to see me succeed at anything!" she pushed him.

"Yeah? Then why was I always encouraging you to write that novel you said you'd always wanted to write?" he challenged.

"Easy. You knew the odds were against me making any kind of real money with it."

He grinned. "You're getting paranoid, hon," he laughed. Then, before she could stop him, he planted a kiss on her cheek and, turning abruptly, walked away.

She started after him, not sure why she was trying so hard to remember how long it had been since he kissed her.

Or why it suddenly made her want to cry.

The call from C. W. Washburn couldn't have come at a better time.

Washburn—nobody knew for sure what the "C.W." stood for—had been the prosecutor on the Rollins case right from the beginning. There had been rumors flying for months that he'd been approached by publishers, that he would write a book on the case once it was over. None of those rumors had been confirmed—until now.

"I've decided to write a book on the Rollins case."

Mel leaned back in the chair across the desk from the prosecutor. "Now there's a big surprise," he commented with mild amusement.

"Then you've heard the rumors."

"Everybody in Saint Louis has heard them, Mr. Washburn," Mel said. "You might as well have bought time on TV."

"I turned down the first offer I received," Washburn explained. "I thought it would be perceived as a conflict of interest—but this latest offer, well, it was just too good to pass on."

"Let me get this straight," Mel said, leaning forward with a knowing smile on his face. "The more money a publisher is willing to pay, the less of a conflict of interest it will be."

The comment obviously stung, as he'd meant it to. Washburn pulled himself upright, his face dark with anger. "I wouldn't be so quick to judge if I were you," he said stiffly. "I asked you here to make you a proposition."

"Hold on." Mel raised a hand to silence him. "If you're going to ask me not to write this—"

"On the contrary, " Washburn said quickly. "I want you to write it—the book, that is."

Mel wasn't sure he'd heard correctly. "I'm afraid I don't understand—"

"I want you to work with me. As a collaborator," Washburn told him.

"Ah," Mel said with a slight nod. This was getting better all the time. "If you don't mind my asking—why me?"

"Why not you? You're a Pulitzer Prize winner, you're with the most powerful paper in town—"

"And I've fried your butt in print a couple of times."

"You're objective."

"You sure you want that much objectivity?"

"Absolutely."

"I'm not one of your biggest fans."

"But you're clearly the best man for the job—and that's all I care about."

"Tell me . . . why do you want a collaborator at all? Why not do it all by yourself and not have to share the money?"

"I'm an attorney, Mr. Riggs, not a writer. Besides, two people working together will speed up the process."

Who are you trying to kid, mister? Mel was thinking. What you want is some flunky to do all the work while you get all the credit. I wasn't born yesterday. "I'll have to think about it," he found himself saying as he got to his feet. "You do know that Kathleen Wilder of the *Daily Mirror* is already under contract to do a book for Pelham and Parker—"

Washburn dismissed the idea with a wave of his hand. "Won't be anything more than a compilation of newspaper stories," he said confidently.

"Yeah, right." Mel started for the door. "I'll get back to you."

"Make it soon," Washburn advised.

"Oh, don't worry about that. It will be. Very soon."

He wouldn't admit it to the other man, but he'd already made up his mind.

Mel thought about it. As much as he hated to admit it, Kathy was right. Richard was right. Everybody was right. And he was only going to agree to this collaboration with Washburn because of Kathy's plans.

She'd never understood because he'd never been able to tell her about his mother, about the first woman who'd ever walked out on him—when he was just a kid. He'd never been able to talk about his mother, a selfish, ambitious woman who'd been willing to give up her own child to make a name for herself. What kind of woman walked out on her own kid? He'd never been able to figure that one out. All those years, and she'd never called, never written to see how he was doing. He could have died, and she never would have known.

Fifteen years ago he found out she was living in New York, editor of one of the top women's magazines. It figured. She'd remarried but had no children. That didn't surprise him. He'd made no attempt to contact her. *She didn't want me then, I don't want her now,* he reasoned.

It did turn him off ambitious women. He'd sworn he'd never marry a career woman—but when he met Kathy, well, everything had happened so quickly and he'd fallen so hard for her, he hadn't realized how important her work was to her.

Until it was too late.

Two days later Mel telephoned C. W. Washburn. "I've given a lot of thought to your proposition," he said, bypassing the usual—and in this case, unnecessary—amenities.

"And?"

"I'm taking you up on your offer."

Three

"I don't want this to go public for a while yet," Washburn told Mel at the prosecutor's office the next morning. "I'm sure I don't have to tell you why."

Mel nodded, refraining from saying what he was thinking, which would have most certainly been taken as another smart-ass remark on his part. "Conflict of interest again," he said with remarkable restraint.

Washburn frowned. "If Preston gets hold of this, he'll move heaven and hell to get me taken off the case. He'll cry foul to every judge and reporter within a hundred-mile radius." Preston was J. L. Preston, the defense attorney who had the instincts of a great white shark and a reputation to match.

Mel turned it over in his mind for a moment. "I wouldn't be at all surprised." It struck him now that, though he'd seen C. W. Washburn at least a hundred times and knew he was no Cary Grant, he hadn't realized until this moment just how much the prosecutor resembled a walrus. Put tusks on him and the picture's complete, Mel thought, amused.

"Can you take a leave of absence?" Washburn was asking.

"I beg your pardon?" Mel wasn't sure he'd heard correctly.

"A leave of absence—can you get one?"

Mel laughed aloud at the thought. "You've got to be kidding!"

"It would only be for six months—eight at the most," Washburn said matter-of-factly. "Time is of the utmost importance now, especially with another book in the works."

Mel grinned. "I thought you weren't worried about Kathy Wilder."

"I said her book would be a compilation of newspaper stories," Washburn corrected. "But I

still don't want her book out there ahead of mine—
ours. I don't have to tell you that the first book out
will be the one making the most money."

"You don't have to tell me a lot of things, Mr.
Washburn." Mel paused. "Just what kind of time-
table are we looking at here, anyway?" He leaned
back in the chair, propping his sneaker-clad feet on
the corner of the prosecutor's antique oak desk.

"Get your feet off the desk, Riggs. It's an antique," Washburn growled, making a sweeping
motion with his hand. "I figure we need a complete manuscript by late May, early June."

"That'll be tough," Mel said, shaking his head.

"But it can be done."

"Oh, sure—it can be done," Mel acknowledged. "If you're prepared to work round-the-
clock, seven days a week, it can be done."

"If you were to take a leave—"

Mel waved him off. "No can do," he insisted.
"Call it human weakness, but I've developed a few
rather nasty habits I can't seem to break. I like to
eat. I like having a roof over my head. And I really
like not having bill collectors beating down my
door."

"We *will* be getting an advance from the publisher," Washburn reminded him.

"Yeah? How much?"

Washburn quoted a figure.

"How much up front?"

"About half."

"And what's my cut?"

"We'll work all of that out—"

"We'll work it out before I put pen to notebook," Mel told him firmly. "I'll have to have a collaboration agreement—you know, one of those legal things that spells out who does what and gets what. Just so there are no misunderstandings, you understand."

Washburn gave him a knowing smile. "What's the matter, Melvin—don't you trust me?"

"No, offense, Mr. Washburn," Mel answered carefully, "but business is business, and I'd want it in writing even if I were dealing with old Abe Lincoln himself."

"Have you heard the rumors?" Darcy wanted to know.

"That's what I like about you, Darcy," Kathleen said with a laugh as she settled into the booth across from her friend at Union Station's Fedora Café. "You get right to the point. No 'hello,' no 'how are you,' just get on to the main event, put all the cards on the table and all that."

"Well, have you?" Darcy asked again, impatiently.

"Have I what?"

"Heard the rumors." Darcy looked as if she might reach across the table and strangle Kathleen at any moment.

"Rumors? What rumors?"

"Oh, come *on*, Kathy!" Darcy shrieked, so loudly that every diner within earshot turned around. "There're rumors flying all over town that Washburn's made a deal for a book and that he's got a local reporter working with him on it."

Oh, she'd heard the rumors, all right. She would have had to have spent the past three weeks in Siberia not to have heard them. "I've heard," she said aloud, "but I wouldn't be at all surprised if Washburn had started those rumors himself, that egomaniac."

"What about the rumors that the reporter in question is none other than your ex-husband?" Darcy asked.

Kathleen shrugged. "They're two of a kind. They deserve each other."

Darcy, looking past Kathleen to the entrance, let out a low whistle. "Speak of the devil," she said, lowering her voice considerably. "Guess who just walked in?"

Kathleen glanced over her shoulder. "Great. Just what I need to ruin my appetite."

It was Mel.

"He's coming this way," Darcy said then.

He'd spotted Kathleen at the same time she saw him and was picking his way through the maze of tables and booths, coming toward her. "Well, well—Kathy Wilder, of all people," he greeted her. "I thought you'd be home, chained to your computer—or don't you have a deadline anymore?"

"I've got a deadline," she said tightly, infuriated by the grin on his face. Infuriated by the sight of him, as long as she was being honest with herself. "I do, however, have to eat."

"Yeah? And all this time I had you figured to be one of those gals who lived on sprouts and seaweed."

"You mean health food," she said, fuming.

His grin widened. "Nothing could stay healthy on that stuff, honey," he said with a wink that drove her straight up the wall. "Got to go—I see my date over there." As he walked away, he called over his shoulder, "Keep in touch, babe."

Her face was dark with rage as she watched him go. "I'd like to touch—"

Darcy grabbed her arm then. "Kathy—look! Look who he's meeting!"

Kathleen frowned as she saw Riggs seat himself at a table across the room.

His "date" was C. W. Washburn.

"We're not going to be able to keep this under wraps much longer," Mel told Washburn. "The rumors are already all over town. I even heard it mentioned on TV last night."

Washburn nodded. "I'm meeting with the state's attorney to discuss it tomorrow morning," he said. "Tomorrow afternoon, I'll make a statement to the press. You'll be there, of course."

Mel grinned. "Wouldn't miss it for the world." There was a pause. "Think you'll get booted off the case?"

Washburn shrugged. "I'd bet any amount of money Preston will do whatever it takes to have me removed." He took a deep breath. "It would be to our advantage if I stay on it, but I can handle it if I should be removed."

Mel scratched the back of his head in a gesture that suggested he didn't know what else to do with his hand. "Can't say I'd blame him—under the circumstances."

"You don't like me very much," Washburn observed dispassionately. "Will that be a problem for you—working with me, I mean?"

"Nah," Mel said with a dismissive wave of his hand. "I've worked with people I didn't like before."

He saw no reason to elaborate on it, to tell Washburn that he disliked him more than most. But it was the truth.

"I'm going to take a leave of absence," Kathleen told Darcy.

"Will they allow that?" Darcy bit into a piece of hot bread and chewed thoughtfully. "I mean, can you take six months off and then go back to the paper at the end of that time, just like that?"

"Not 'just like that,' no," Kathleen admitted. "I probably won't get my spot in features back—I'd probably end up on general assignment again. I'm going to talk to my editor, day after tomorrow. This happens at the *Star* all the time—somebody's always writing a book over there—but nobody's ever done it before at the *Daily Mirror.* They may not go for it at all."

"And if they don't?" Darcy asked.

Kathleen gave a little shrug. "I guess I'll quit."

Kathleen lay awake that night, remembering things she wished she could forget. Things she knew she'd be better off forgetting. Silly things, really. She was thinking about Mel, about how wonderful it had been for them once and how much it had hurt to have to end it.

But it had been so good in the beginning....

"Hey, Kathy—where are you?"

"You bellowed?"

Kathy went into the living room of the small house she and Mel had rented in Paw Paw, just a few miles west of Kalamazoo. She'd been in the kitchen, attempting to pull together a potluck dinner when he came home, and looked as if she'd been fighting a losing battle with it. There was flour on her baggy shirt and on the tip of her nose. Her jeans were ripped at the knees, and her hair was pulled back in a ponytail from which a few strands of hair had escaped.

He grinned. "Jeez, honey—you look great," he told her.

"Smart aleck," she scolded playfully. "What've you got behind your back?"

"A Valentine's Day present." He still wouldn't let her see it.

"For me?"

"No—it's for Mrs. Abraham next door—of course it's for you, silly!" he chuckled.

"Well, as it happens, I have something for you, too," she told him, trying to get around him to get a better look at the package.

He sidestepped her easily. "Yeah? What is it?"

"It's a surprise."

"Oh, good. I've been needing one of those." He produced the package at last—a large, heart-shaped box adorned with red silk roses. "Happy Valentine's Day, babe."

She grabbed the box and opened it hastily. "Mel, you nut! This is just—" She stopped short when she saw the contents of the box. "You're kidding!"

Inside the box was a skimpy, nearly transparent, blue silk teddy. It was going to be great with the skimpy black briefs she'd gotten him.

Mel grinned.

"You've done so well on your diet. Couldn't very well bring you candy."

"Right. You would have had to eat it."

A big smile came to his lips. "Maybe I should've taken those Godivas, after all."

"Now how did I know you'd say that?"

"Because," he said, pulling her close, "you know me so well."

He kissed her long and hard. She wrapped her arms around him, returning his kisses with equal enthusiasm. Then, abruptly, he scooped her up into his arms and carried her into their bedroom. "Wait a minute." She giggled. "Just what have you got in mind here?"

He grinned. "What do you think?"

"It's still early," she pointed out feebly.

"You on a time clock or something?" He started taking off his shirt.

"No, but I do have dinner in the oven—"

"It'll keep."

"It'll burn."

"Let it."

"The house, too?"

"Why not? It's not ours."

"But we're in it."

"Good point." He joined her on the bed. "We'll have to make it fast."

She laughed. "Rats!"

He kissed her again, hovering over her as he unbuttoned her shirt. "Well . . . maybe not *too* fast," he said as he unfastened the front closure of her lacy white bra and stroked her breasts. "How long do we have before the kitchen goes up in a blaze of unglory?"

"Forty-five minutes. At least."

"Long enough." He stood to finish taking off his own clothes, never taking his eyes off her while she wriggled out of her jeans and panties.

He had such a good body, she thought as she looked up at him. She'd always been a little insecure about her own unclothed body—but he took such obvious pleasure in it that she'd become much less critical of herself lately. But Mel...Mel looked soooo good....

Not an ounce of spare flesh anywhere on his body, she observed. All lean and muscular. And all mine, she thought possessively.

He came back to her, lying beside her on the bed. Instantly they were in each other's arms, kissing, touching each other everywhere. Arms and legs entwined, they melted together in the heat of passion. His lips seemed to be everywhere at once—on her face, her neck, her breasts. She closed her eyes, giving herself up to the sensations he stirred deep within her core...of his lips on her breast, nuzzling, kissing, sucking...she felt his hand on the inside of her thigh, stroking, moving upward slowly, deliberately...then he was touching her *there,* his fingertips brushing her lightly, then insistently, driving her wild with need.

"Oh, Mel..." she moaned. "Now...."

He stopped what he was doing abruptly and raised his head to kiss her again, at first lightly, fleetingly, then again, more insistently, more hungrily. Then again, long and deep and hard.

She gave a little moan. "Now, Mel," she breathed. "Now, please...."

He shook his head emphatically. "No, not yet." He ran his thumb slowly across her lips, still wet and swollen from that last hard kiss. She didn't understand. She could tell by his ragged breath, by the tautness of his body on top of hers, that he was barely able to control his own need. Why didn't he give in to it? Why didn't he give in to hers?

His fingers were in her hair, gently pulling her head back. Her throat arched and more accessible to his lips now, he let them trail over the smooth flesh lazily, teasing, tantalizing her. He nuzzled her ear, then the base of her neck. His fingers skimmed her flesh as he lowered his head to her breast again, his mouth tugging at her nipple with just enough force to elicit a tingle deep within her. Then he rolled over, taking her with him, landing on his back with Kathleen on top of him. She fingered the pelt of hair that covered his chest as she planted random kisses on his shoulders and collarbone. His fingers were touching, probing, sending something very much like an electrical current coursing through her. "Now, Mel...."

Then he was inside her, and they were moving together to a wild, primitive rhythm. She was swept away on the current of her own desire, and he followed closely behind her. She felt his body begin to shudder violently, then relax.

"Now I know why I married you," he gasped breathlessly.

She gave him a lazy smile as she stroked his head.
"And why is that?" she asked dreamily.

"Because we fit together so well."

She laughed. "Now why doesn't that comment
surprise me?" she wondered aloud.

He raised his head to kiss her full on the mouth.
"Because you know me so well...."

I thought I did, anyway, she thought now as a
tear rolled down her cheek. But I wonder if I ever
really knew you at all. But the inescapable truth was
that Darcy had been right.

She was still in love with him.

Across town, Mel, finding himself sleeping
alone—though not by choice—was also reliving old
times. Recalling happier times. Funny... when he
and Kathy were first married, they didn't have
much; they'd barely managed to make ends meet in
spite of the fact that they were both working full-
time—but they'd been happy. Oh, they'd had their
share of squabbles, but somehow they hadn't
seemed so important then....

"The refrigerator's on the blink again, Mel,"
Kathleen told him. "Take a look at it, will you?"

He made a face. "What do I look like—the
Frigidaire man?"

"Get serious, Riggs," she scolded him.

"I am. I don't know the first thing about these contraptions."

"We can't afford a repairman. You'll have to do whatever you can."

"Okay, okay. But no promises, okay?"

"Fair enough."

She hadn't complained, even when he was able to barely keep the thing running. "Soon we'll be able to buy a new one," she'd predicted.

Then the washing machine she'd bought at a yard sale stopped working.

"Just look at it, okay?" she pleaded.

"What do I look like, the Maytag repairman?"

"I'm beginning to think you're a stand-up comic," she shot back at him. "Just get the washer going, will you? I can't even think about having to go to the Laundromat after work once a week."

But she had gone to the Laundromat—for the next three weeks. And never complained once.

"I got the fridge and the washer fixed," she told him one night.

"Yeah? How'd you do that?"

"The man down the street. Mr. Halsey. I ran into him at the post office, we got to talking, and he said he'd take a look at them."

"The big, good-looking guy? The one who looks like he should be doing ads for underwear?"

"That's the one."

"What did it cost us?"

"Nothing."

He shot her a suspicious look.

She tried not to smile. "He said I could either bake him a cake or sleep with him."

"And?"

"Who do I look like—the Galloping Gourmet?"

"That does it, woman!" he roared, advancing on her menacingly. They both broke into a run. He chased her into the bedroom, pinning her down on the bed.

"You're not mad, are you?" she gasped, giggling uncontrollably.

"Darn right I am. Now I know why you never baked *me* a cake...."

She'd delighted in teasing him like that he now recalled, at least in the beginning. That's all it was. Kathy would have died before she let another man touch her.

We were so good together, Kathy, he thought. We could have been so good....but we never really had a chance, did we?

Kathleen knew something important was going on the minute she walked into the *Daily Mirror* newsroom on Thursday morning. Had she not been so nervous about the talk she was planning to have with her editor, she might have been curious enough to join the group of reporters engaged in a rather animated conversation around the water cooler on the other side of the room—a group that became strangely silent when they saw her.

"Is Gerry in?" she asked the secretary, a heavy-set, middle-aged woman who'd been with the paper three times as long as she had—and would probably still be there when Kathleen was ready for retirement.

The woman shook her head. "He called ten minutes ago, said he'd be in by noon. Car trouble, I think."

Of all days, Kathleen thought, frustrated. "Okay," she said aloud. "Tell him I really have to talk to him, so he shouldn't leave this evening till I get back."

The woman nodded. "I guess having such formidable competition is putting you under a lot of pressure," she said then.

Kathleen stopped in her tracks. "I beg your pardon?"

"Oh—you haven't heard." The other woman looked more concerned than surprised.

"Heard what?"

"It was in Harold Gresham's column this morning. Melvin Riggs and C. W. Washburn—they're working together on a book. On the Rollins case. They've got a contract."

I knew it, Kathleen thought angrily as she walked into the ladies' room on the ground floor of the county courthouse. Nobody thought he was interested in doing a book, but I knew it.

Well, I'll show him. I'll show both of them.

She spotted him the minute she walked out of the rest room. He was on the other side of the busy lobby, leaned up against the wall, looking cocky as ever. It was almost as if he'd been waiting for her there.

Well, I'm not going to let him get to me, she thought, pulling herself up straight as she marched toward him, her right hand extended. "I hear congratulations are in order."

He looked slightly bewildered as he shook her hand. "Well—thanks."

"Who's your agent?" she asked pleasantly.

"Uh—Patrick Vesper. Actually, he's Washburn's agent, but since we're working together, well, you know." He looked as though he expected her to attack him at any moment. "Who's yours?"

"Carla Phillips."

"I hear she's good." He took a feeble stab at small talk. "How'd you get her?"

"Through a friend. She was her agent, so Darcy put me in touch."

He nodded. "I see."

This was ridiculous! "Look," Kathleen said finally, "since we're obviously going to be competing with each other again, we might as well accept it. We should be used to it by now."

He nodded again. "May the best man win and all that?"

She laughed. "Not a chance!" Then, impulsively, she reached out and gave his shoulder a friendly pat. "See you at the finish line, Melvin. Hope you like the taste of dust."

Four

———

Mel suppressed a smile as he watched her disappear into the crowd now entering the courtroom. Didn't she realize how obvious she was? he wondered. The book deal didn't mean anything to her. She was only interested in finally beating him at something—anything. And he'd only made matters worse by competing with her.

It wasn't always like this, he thought with a sudden twinge of sadness. There was a time...ah, what's the use? That's history. After all these years, there's not much point in worrying about it.

So why did it still bother him?

He pushed those thoughts to the back of his mind and fell in line behind other reporters entering the courtroom. If it's competition she wants, he was thinking, it's competition she'll get.

There were at least a dozen reporters from local newspapers and TV stations clustered together in the press section. No photographers were allowed, but Mel recognized at least two well-known artists who frequently did courtroom illustrations. The one from the *Daily Mirror* was a good-looking, single man in his late thirties who bore an uncanny resemblance to Tom Selleck—right down to the mustache.

Mel wondered if Kathy had ever gone out with him.

If she did, it's none of your business, he scolded himself. You're divorced, remember?

How could you forget?

He found a seat—and found himself sitting directly behind Kathleen, who hadn't noticed. She was talking to the woman seated to her right, another reporter for the *Daily Mirror*.

What did they do, send their entire staff? he wondered. Then he remembered that Kathleen was no longer covering the case for her paper. Just as he no longer covered it for his.

A reporter for one of the out-of-town papers, a fairly pleasant fellow Mel had met once or twice before, squeezed in and seated himself between Mel and one of the TV people.

"I feel like I've been driving all day and all night," he confided to Mel. "Couldn't even get a room at the motel."

Mel grinned. "You must've gotten there about the time the lunch crowd was checking in."

The other man gave him a puzzled look.

Mel's grin vanished abruptly. "Never mind."

"I hope I can get a room here in town."

"Shouldn't be too much of a problem, Mel told him.

"I haven't even been able to change my shirt."

At that, everyone seated on either side of him moved away abruptly.

"Nice going," Mel told him. "Good way to get a little more elbow room."

The other man's face flushed noticeably.

Mel patted his shoulder. "Hey—whatever works, right?"

He turned his attention back to the front of the courtroom—or more precisely, to the row of spectators directly in front of him. Kathleen was talking to the Tom Selleck clone. She was smiling. Of course she was smiling—the jerk was acting as though she was the only woman on the planet! What red-blooded woman in her right mind wouldn't smile?

Has she got something going with him? Mel wondered again.

Kathleen could tell her ex-husband was annoyed. And she was enjoying every minute of it.

Let him sweat, she thought, leaning forward just a little to make their conversation appear more intimate than it actually was. For Mel's benefit, she deliberately reached up and put a hand on David's shoulder, then leaned close to confide a funny story to him. They laughed together, and out of the corner of her eye she could see Mel fuming.

Good, she thought. It was nice to know she could still get to him.

The courtroom was called to order. As the prosecution called the first witness of the day, Kathleen found herself studying C. W. Washburn intently. The man looked like a walrus. The longer she looked at him, the clearer the resemblance was. She tried not to laugh. It was getting harder and harder to imagine him and Mel working together. They had absolutely nothing in common.

She glanced over her shoulder. Behind her, Mel was furiously taking notes. "Damn!" he muttered under his breath when his ballpoint pen ran out of ink. He checked all of his pockets but didn't have another.

"Here," said Kathleen, offering him one of hers.

He looked at her, slightly bewildered for a moment, then took it. "Thanks," he said finally.

She smiled sweetly. "Believe me, it's my pleasure." She turned her attention back to the front of the courtroom until, a few seconds later, the sounds of muffled expletives behind her told her he'd discovered why she'd been so generous.

The pen she'd given him leaked!

She bit her lower lip to keep from laughing aloud as she saw him, out of the corner of her eye, jump to his feet and rush out of the courtroom, his shirt and hands spotted with blue ink.

That's one for the home team, she thought smugly.

"So you want to play dirty, do you?" Mel muttered angrily as he bent over the sink in the men's room, trying in vain to scrub the ink off his hands. "Okay, lady, I'll play dirty with you. You bet I'll play dirty!"

As he raised his eyes to the mirror over the sink, he caught sight of a man coming out of one of the stalls, looking at him oddly. Mel grinned. "I talk to myself all the time," he said cheerfully. "My shrink

says I've done it ever since I went off the deep end
and took an ax to my ex-wife.''

The other man, looking horrified, backed away.
He scurried out the door, and Mel turned back to
the mirror. He was smiling.

"Take an ax to my ex-wife," he said to himself.
"What an appealing idea!"

Carol was asleep.

The reporter officially covering the Rollins case
for the *Daily Mirror* had gone to sleep—right there
in the courtroom. Kathleen had nudged her several
times to bring her around—but now she was not
only asleep but snoring.

Snoring!

Kathleen was mortified. Several of the jurors
were looking in their direction, as was Washburn,
who'd been interrupted midsentence by the un-
earthly sounds coming from the press section. She
was so embarrassed she didn't see Mel return to the
courtroom until he was behind her.

"Jeez, Kathy—you must be a brilliant conver-
sationalist," he whispered, "if you're putting them
to sleep now."

"Shut up—*Melvin,*" she shot back at him.

"Don't you think you should wake her up?"

"Don't you think you should mind your own
business?" she growled.

"I think it's become the business of everyone within earshot," he said, loudly enough that he could be heard as well.

Kathleen wanted to kill him. But even more than that, she wanted to crawl under the bench and hide.

I'd kill him—if I could find some silver bullets!

Kathleen threw her bag down on the couch and kicked off her shoes with such force that the heel of one made a small hole in the wall when it hit.

I've never been so embarrassed in my life. And he was enjoying every minute of it.

Just thinking about it raised her blood pressure. Just thinking about *him* raised her blood pressure. Many more days in the same courtroom with him, she thought angrily, and I'll have a stroke! He'd probably love that.

She took off her yellow linen jacket and dropped it over the back of a nearby chair. If only she'd known he was here before she took the job at the paper. She wouldn't have come within a hundred miles of Saint Louis. But now that she was here, she was going to have to make the best of it.

Make the best of it. That's a laugh.

Maybe I could get the paper to send me somewhere as a special correspondent. Someplace more peaceful than this.

Like Beirut.

*   *   *

"Please—don't send Carol again," Kathleen pleaded. "She fell asleep in the courtroom yesterday!"

"It's her story," Gerry Hancock reminded her. "Besides, it wasn't the first time a court reporter fell asleep during the proceedings. Chances are nobody noticed."

"Everybody noticed," Kathleen assured him. "She was snoring, Gerry."

The editor gave her a disbelieving look. "You're kidding."

Kathleen made a face. "Would I make jokes about such things?"

Gerry shook his head. "Lately, you don't joke about much of anything," he pointed out.

"These days, the business isn't much of a laughing matter," she said wearily, dropping into a chair in front of the editor's desk.

"The Rollins case is getting to you, is it?" Gerry was only half listening as he sorted through his telephone messages.

"No. Melvin Riggs is getting to me," she answered honestly. "I think he was put on this earth to make my life hell." Normally she would not have told an editor—any editor—that a reporter from a rival newspaper who just happened to be her ex-husband was making her life miserable, but Gerry wasn't just an editor, he was a friend. He understood.

"Nonsense," Gerry growled. "He makes your life hell because you let him make it hell."

"Believe me, he's got a real talent for it." She paused momentarily. "But that's not why I'm here."

"You're here because tomorrow's your last day," he concluded.

"Well—yes."

He nodded. "You *are* still coming back after the book's finished—" he started.

"Definitely," she said quickly. "I love my work, Gerry. I'm going to miss it."

"For the most part, anyway."

"I won't have the opportunity to miss my ex-husband," she said regretfully. "Not that I ever would, but I have a feeling I'll be seeing more of Mel Riggs than ever."

The editor hesitated for a moment. "Whatever came between you two, anyway?" he asked finally.

"Ego. *His* ego, to be precise." She stood up. "Look, Gerry, I've got to run. I have an interview at ten. I just wanted to touch base."

"Your job will be here when you're ready to come back," he reassured her.

"Thanks," she said, winking as she opened the door. "Between you and me, I'll probably need it."

"How long a leave of absence are we talking about?" Bill Richfield, the editor-in-chief of the *Star* wanted to know.

"Six months. Maybe less. Probably less." Mel leaned back in his seat and irreverently propped his sneaker-clad feet on the desk. "All I need is enough time to finish the manuscript."

"Get your feet off my desk," the editor ordered sharply as he flipped through the pages of his desk calendar and made some notations. "That means you'll be back in late August."

Mel obeyed the order quickly. "That sounds about right."

"I don't see any problem with that." Richfield turned the calendar back to the current date. "I take it you want it to commence immediately."

"If that's possible."

The editor nodded. "A little unorthodox, but I have no problem with it if the guys upstairs don't," he said. "I'll let you know if they do."

Mel grinned. "They'll probably be glad to be rid of me."

Richfield didn't look up from the notes he was making on a yellow legal pad. "I don't know about *them,* but *I* will be," he said soberly.

Mel wasn't sure if he was kidding or not.

"I thought real women didn't pump gas."

Kathleen looked up to see Mel standing on the other side of the gas pump. "If I don't do it, it doesn't get done," she responded coldly.

You, of all people, should know that, she was thinking.

"You always did want to be independent," Mel recalled with a smile that bordered on a smirk.

You always had to prove you could do anything a man can do, he thought.

"I've learned the hard way that the only person I can really depend on is myself," she said tightly as she replaced the cap on her gas tank. *I sure couldn't depend on you.*

He leaned against the gas pump, watching her. "Nobody ever said you couldn't take care of yourself," he said. *And you took care of me in the process—boy, did you take care of me!*

"I was under the impression you thought I needed to be taken care of." *You sure didn't act like you thought I was capable of doing anything by myself.*

"I would have liked to at least think I was taking care of you," he admitted. *But it would have been like trying to take care of Attila the Hun.*

"Translated, you wanted me to be dependent on you." *And boost your male ego in the process.*

"Perish the thought!" *If war broke out tomorrow, you'd probably be right out there on the front lines.*

She pushed past him. "I think I'd better get out of here before I say something I'll regret," she snapped. *Fat chance!*

"You? Regret anything?" He laughed aloud at the thought. *Fat chance!*

He watched her go off to pay for her gas. It reminded him of another time, another place.

He was thinking of the day they met.

She was mad at him then, too.

"You two should make a serious effort to bury the hatchet," Richard advised.

"Oh, she'd love to," Mel said, thumbing through his telephone messages before tackling the pile of mail on his desk. "What worries me is *where she'd like to bury it.*"

"I'm serious."

"So am I."

"You ought to try to make peace with him," Darcy told Kathleen.

"I'd like to make pieces of him," Kathleen grumbled.

"You must have loved him once," Darcy maintained, picking at her lunch.

"I thought I did," Kathleen said sullenly. "I was mistaken."

I did love him once. But I was young and foolish then. I didn't know any better.

Before, Kathleen thought of Mel only occasionally, usually late at night when she was alone and wishing she wasn't. Mostly she'd wondered if he was dead or alive. With Mel's penchant for getting into trouble, one could never be sure. She remembered one incident when they were still married and living in Michigan....

"She's been missing two weeks now," Mel said, staring at the TV screen. "I was assigned to cover the story. I was doing my job. That's all."

She gave a little laugh as she rumpled his hair and moved closer to him on the couch. "Hey—you don't have to convince me," she reminded him. "I've been there, remember?"

"No, honey, you've never been *here* before," he said grimly, still staring at the man being interviewed on TV. "That's her husband. He claims the story I wrote could cause her death."

She gave him a puzzled look. "Her death? How?"

"She's been kidnapped. He thinks my story gave away too much about police efforts to get the kidnappers."

Kathleen thought about it for a moment. "What would you do if I were kidnapped?" she wanted to know.

"Sit back and wait."

She sat up and looked at him. *"What?"*

"I'd wait to see how much they'd pay me to take you back."

"You louse!" She hit him with a pillow.

He grabbed her wrists, laughing. "See what I mean?" he asked, pulling her down across his lap. "They wouldn't keep you twenty-four hours. You're too much trouble."

She pulled his face down to hers for a long, delicious kiss. "Tell me," she murmured against his lips, "if I ever *were* kidnapped, would you pay to get me back?"

He kissed her again. "Every cent I have," he assured her.

Kathleen giggled. "And what would you tell them when they stopped laughing?" she wanted to know.

It was hard to believe things could have been so good between them then and so tense now, Kathleen thought with a twinge of bitterness. I did love him then, she thought, but I was young and foolish and didn't know any better.

So what's my excuse now?

Five

"How is the book coming along?"

"Slowly," Kathleen admitted as she walked through the busy main terminal at Lambert-Saint Louis International Airport with Carla Phillips, who was making a stopover in Saint Louis to see Kathleen en route to the West Coast for a meeting with a producer with whom she was negotiating a motion picture deal. "It's a lot different from writing newspaper stories—more so than I expected."

Carla didn't seem too concerned. "There's always an adjustment to be made when one switches medias," she said as they positioned themselves near the baggage carousel to wait for her luggage.

Kathleen hesitated, not sure she wanted Carla to know the whole story. "There's more to it than just switching medias," she said finally.

Carla raised an eyebrow questioningly. "Oh?"

"You *do* know there's another book on this case under contract," Kathleen said, unable to imagine that she might not know. It seemed to her that Carla knew everything that went on in the business.

"I'm aware of it, yes," Carla said with a nod. "The author is the prosecutor assigned to the case, is he not?"

"Yeah." Kathleen paused. "His coauthor is a reporter for another Saint Louis newspaper."

"Yes, I'd heard that."

"He's also my ex-husband."

Carla, who'd bent to retrieve one of her bags from the carousel, stopped what she was doing and straightened up abruptly. "Melvin Riggs is your ex-husband?" she asked.

Kathleen made a wry face. "Yeah. The Pulitzer Prize winner was married to an anonymous reporter for a small-time paper," she said with a trace of resentment in her voice.

"How long have the two of you been divorced?" Carla asked.

Kathleen frowned. "Not nearly long enough."

"This town doesn't seem to be big enough for both of us."

Kathleen almost dropped her fork at the sound of his voice. "I don't believe this," she muttered under her breath as he approached the table where she and Carla were having dinner.

"Who is he?" Carla asked, keeping her voice low.

"My ex-husband—in the flesh." Kathleen turned in her chair to face him. "This used to be a nice restaurant—but they must have lowered their standards if they're letting you in."

Mel grinned. "Flattery will get you everywhere," he said in a teasing tone.

"Not exactly where I'd want to be with you," she shot back at him.

"You didn't always feel that way," he pursued.

"Only after I grew up," Kathleen said crossly.

Mel looked at Carla, who'd been observing them in silence. "I don't believe we've met," he said, extending his hand. "I'm Mel Riggs."

She shook his hand. "Carla Phillips."

He raised an eyebrow. "I've heard a lot about you."

"And I you," Carla told him.

"From her?" He laughed, gesturing toward Kathleen. "I'll just bet you did—but don't believe a word of it!"

"I didn't tell her anything that's not true," Kathleen said coldly.

"From whose point of view?" he wanted to know.

Kathleen's patience was beginning to wear thin. "Are you meeting someone here, *Melvin,* or did you just stop by to ruin my appetite?"

"I've got a date," he said, grinning. "She's running a little late."

"If she's smart, she's running for her life," Kathleen said in a slightly sarcastic tone.

Mel looked at Carla with a conspiratorial smile. "She's jealous," he offered in explanation. "Trouble is, she lets it show."

"Jealous?" Kathleen laughed aloud at the thought. "Only in your dreams!"

He looked up as a tall blond woman in a dress that looked like it had been painted on her voluptuous body came into the restaurant, looking around as though she were lost. "My date's arrived," he said to Kathleen and Carla. "Excuse me?"

"I always have," Kathleen assured him.

He ignored her remark. "See you in court, sweetheart," he called over his shoulder to Kathleen as he walked away.

"Just his type," Kathleen commented, giving the other woman the once-over. "All body and no brains." She turned back to Carla. "Why does love hurt so much when it ends?" she wondered aloud.

"It doesn't," Carla said wisely. "It only hurts when it's still alive."

It only hurts when it's still alive. Just what she needed to hear.

That thought nagged Kathleen the next day as she attempted to review her research. Carla had seen it. And if it were that obvious to a woman who didn't know her all that well on a personal level, how must it look to her friends and colleagues?

How must it look to Mel?

She switched off the tape recorder on her desk. It was no use. She'd run the same tape four times that morning—an interview with a maid at the hotel where June Rollins had died—and she had yet to hear it from start to finish. Her mind kept wandering, straying from the task at hand.

And I thought he'd stop being a thorn in my side the day the divorce became final!

Frustrated, she sat there for a long time, tapping her pen on the desk. How could she still love him?

How could she possibly love such a jerk? But then, he hadn't been a jerk when she married him—or, more precisely, he hadn't been such an obvious jerk. He'd been everything she wasn't—and at the time, that had been exactly what she needed. . . .

"You know what they say about all work and no play," Mel reminded her as he led her into that small park in southwestern Michigan where they'd spent so many happy hours at the beginning of their relationship.

"We'll have plenty of time to play—we're probably going to both have pink slips waiting for us when we get back to the office," Kathleen worried.

"They can't fire us," he said confidently. "Slaves have to be sold."

"Be serious!" Kathleen scolded.

"I *am* serious. Have you taken a look at your paycheck lately?" he wanted to know.

"You must have something on the managing editor," Kathleen concluded, watching as he spread a blanket on the ground and started unpacking the picnic basket he'd brought along.

"Actually," Mel said with a grin. "*He* has something on *me*. Come to think of it, he has a lot on me."

"That's a dangerous position to be in, Riggs," she told him, amused.

"What can I say? I'm a man who likes to live dangerously." He started emptying the contents of a wicker picnic hamper onto the blanket—canned soda, submarine sandwiches, fresh fruit, and cheese cubes.

Kathleen laughed. "You sure came prepared, didn't you?" she asked, scanning the small-scale smorgasbord he'd brought.

"When I do it, I do it right."

"When you do *what?*" she asked suspiciously.

"It. Anything," he said with an impish grin.

"That sounds promising." She settled onto the blanket and accepted the can of soda he offered.

He gave her a sandwich and took one for himself, then sat beside her. Pulling the ring tab to open his own soda, he dropped it into the picnic basket and unwrapped his sandwich. "Hope you like subs," he said, taking a big bite.

"Actually, I usually favor a healthier diet," she admitted.

He looked at her. "You're kidding." He was trying to keep from laughing. "You're a health food nut?"

"I wouldn't put it that way," she said coolly.

"Do you live on nuts and berries?" he wanted to know.

"That *wasn't* what I meant by a healthier diet," she said, somewhat defensively.

"Bean sprouts?"

"You're pushing your luck, Riggs," she warned.

"If you don't like the sub, I can rustle up some tree bark," he offered.

"That's it."

She started to get up, but he grabbed her, pulling her back down, into his arms. When he kissed her, he found her more than receptive. She'd learned a long time ago that it paid to pretend to be angry from time to time...

But by the end, she hadn't been pretending. She *had* been angry. Angry and hurt. The breakup of their marriage had been, without a doubt, the most painful experience of her life.

And to this day, some of the wounds still hadn't healed.

"I'm sorry I didn't get to see Darcy," Carla said, waiting for her flight to be called at the airport the next morning.

"She had to leave rather suddenly," Kathleen said with a knowing smile. "That husband of hers is on the road so much, there's no way she'll ever pass up a chance to join him—no matter where he is.''

Before Carla could respond, her flight was called. As she took her place in line and the passengers started to board, she turned to Kathleen once more. "Remember what I said."

Kathleen gave her a quizzical look.

"Love only hurts when it's still alive."

"Talk about the original odd couple."

Mel looked up from his computer terminal, having barely heard what Richard had just said. "I didn't know we were."

"You and Washburn. The last person on the face of the earth I'd ever expect you to pair off with." He bit into a doughnut. "Doesn't seem possible."

"I'm not marrying the guy, Rich," Mel chuckled. "I'm just writing a book with him."

"From what I hear, that's about the same as being married," Richard observed.

"For six months, I can put up with *anyone*—even C. W. Washburn," Mel said confidently.

Anyone but my ex-wife, he was thinking.

The courtroom was already packed when he arrived the next morning, fifteen minutes late. Court was already in session, and as luck would have it, the only available seat in the press section was directly behind Kathleen.

"Just what I *don't* need," he muttered under his breath as he headed down the aisle.

"Need a pen?" Kathleen asked, looking over her shoulder as he took his seat.

"Nooo, thank you," he responded, shaking his head emphatically. "I brought extras."

"Just thought I'd ask."

"Yeah, right." He paused. "Hey, where's your friend? Did she find a new place to take her afternoon nap?"

"Since I'm no longer actively working for the *Mirror,* I wouldn't know," Kathleen said evenly, "but my guess is that she's on another assignment."

"Seems a shame," Mel said. "She seemed so comfortable here."

"I hope they toss your butt out of here, Riggs." Then, realizing that people were staring, she turned around abruptly, shifting her attention back to the front of the courtroom.

Before they throw both of our butts out of here, she thought.

She wished she could use the tape recorder she used for one-on-one interviews, but she wasn't sure it could pick up the voices of the attorneys and witnesses that far away. And she certainly didn't want her dialogue with Mel on tape.

Looking at C. W. Washburn now, Kathleen still couldn't imagine her ex-husband working with the man—on a book or anything else. Melvin Riggs just wasn't a team player. He worked alone, and that was the way he liked it. He did his best work when he soloed. He could have done the book without Washburn.

And, as much as she hated to admit it, he probably would have done a much better job.

"Rollins was from Dallas," Mel told Richard, sitting in the *Star*'s employee cafeteria. "Most of his family still lives there."

"So?"

"*So?*" Mel laughed. "Jeez, Rich, I'm cutting but you're not bleeding! How'd you ever make it as a reporter?"

"I didn't," Richard said with an offhanded shrug. "That's why they made me a columnist. So what's your point?"

"Rollins was from Dallas." Mel finished his candy bar and wadded the wrapper into a small foil ball. "Unless I dig into his background, talk to the people who knew him when, the book's not going to be complete, right?"

"I guess not."

Mel grinned, patting Richard's shoulder as he pushed his chair away from the table and got to his feet. "That's what I like about you, Rich," he chuckled. "You catch on so fast."

"Why do you want to go to Dallas?" Darcy wanted to know.

"I don't *want* to go," Kathleen said as she packed a suitcase. "I *have* to go."

"All right, then—why do you *have* to go?"

"To look into Rollins's background—you know, find out if he hated his mother or was rejected by his first love, things like that." Kathleen scanned the room in search of a scarf she'd managed to misplace in just a matter of minutes.

Darcy handed it to her. "You're going to play shrink, then."

"No true crime book is good without an in-depth portrait of the accused killer," Kathleen reminded the novelist who had never written a nonfiction book. "To do that in this case, I have to go to Dallas—learn about his past, his family, his marriage—"

"In other words, find out what made him want to kill his wife," Darcy concluded.

Kathleen made a face. "That's the only thing I *don't* need to ask about."

* * *

"Look, I don't have time to explain—they're calling my flight," Mel said irritably. "I'll fill you in when I get back."

He was calling Washburn from a pay phone at the airport. "This is supposed to be a collaboration, Riggs. You're not supposed to do things like this without checking with me first!"

"Listen—I'm not in the habit of letting an editor tell me how to do my job, and I'm not going to let you do it, either!" Mel snapped, slamming the receiver down on its cradle so forcefully that almost everyone within earshot turned to look at him. He paid no attention, stalking off to the gate to board his flight.

This was one day Kathleen would like to forget.

Her alarm hadn't gone off this morning—God only knew why—and she'd overslept. She woke less than an hour before she had to leave for the airport. Rushing around frantically in order to be ready to leave on time, she'd ruined two pair of pantyhose and broken a heel. When she was finally ready to go, she found she'd misplaced her keys.

When she at last found the keys, she rushed out to her car—only to find it had a flat tire. By the time she got the tire changed and changed her clothes—again—she estimated that she had just enough time to get to the airport. But traffic was heavier than usual—heavy even for the morning rush hour on Interstate 70—and she'd reached the gate just as the plane was taking off.

The walk back to the TWA ticket counter was so long, she half expected to be stopped by the border patrol. The man at the ticket counter had tried to be helpful, even though she hadn't been in the most pleasant mood.

"I can put you on standby for the next flight," he offered.

"You do that," she snapped crossly.

What else can go wrong? she wondered now, as she headed back to the gate to wait.

They never take off on time, Mel thought irritably, glancing at his watch. This flight was already running forty minutes behind schedule. It looked as though everyone had boarded—there were only a few empty seats remaining—so what was holding them up?

A flight attendant offered him his choice of a magazine from a large stack. He shook his head, sending her on her way. He wasn't in the mood for reading. Actually he wasn't in much of a mood for anything. Least of all sitting in a cramped seat waiting for a plane to take off that should have taken off forty minutes ago.

He tried to remember the longest wait he'd ever had for a flight to depart.

Thank God for cancellations, Kathleen thought, standing at the counter next to the gate waiting for the attendant to issue her ticket for this flight. She might make it to Dallas today after all.

She gathered up her carry-on luggage and took off through the jetway to board the plane, confident the worst was behind her.

After all, what else could go wrong?

Mel was wondering exactly the same thing when he looked up and saw her standing in the aisle—glaring at him.

"Jeez—are you following me?" he asked incredulously.

"Only in your dreams," she assured him as she stowed her carry-on in the overhead luggage compartment. Then she pulled out her ticket. "I'm afraid there's a mistake here," she informed him coldly.

"I'll say there is!"

"I'm serious, *Melvin,*" she insisted impatiently. "You're in my seat."

"I'm—what?"

"You're in my seat. 22A. I was assigned the window seat," she said, gesturing with her ticket in hand.

"Jeez, are you going to make an issue of it?" he grumbled, ducking his head as he got to his feet and stepped into the aisle.

She didn't respond as she squeezed past him and took her seat next to the window. He settled in next to her and signaled the flight attendant who'd approached him earlier.

"I think I'll have that magazine now," he told her.

"Of course." She showed him the remaining choices, having already distributed more than half of the stack among the other passengers. He chose one; then she turned to Kathleen. "Would you like one?"

Kathleen shook her head. "No, thank you."

As the flight attendant walked away, Mel turned to Kathleen. "So—what are you going to Dallas for?" he asked. *As if I didn't know.*

"Probably for the same reason you are," she said. *As if you had to ask.*

"Maybe we should work together on this," he suggested. *You could see a real pro at work.*

"You mean team up so we'd get finished faster?" she asked. *What you really mean is I'd do all the leg work and you'd take credit for it.*

"Exactly." *It would save me a lot of time and keep you out of the way.*

"I don't think so." *When what freezes over?*

Six

"That's mine," Kathleen said quickly, snatching the suitcase from Mel as he lifted it from the baggage carousel.

He looked at her. "How can you be so sure?" he demanded. "It looks just like mine—or any one of a dozen others on this carousel, for that matter."

"I know—that's why I marked mine," she replied disdainfully.

He released the suitcase abruptly. "Marked it, huh? Now there's a real original idea," he said, grinning for a reason she'd never suspect.

* * *

"I don't believe this!" Kathleen spit, standing on the curb waiting for the hotel shuttle to arrive. Mel had joined the line, obviously enjoying the fact that, of all the hotels in Dallas, they'd somehow ended up at the same one.

"I see we still have the same taste in some things," he joked.

"We never had the same taste in anything," she shot back at him.

"Then how do you explain our having the same luggage?" he wanted to know.

Now he was making fun of her! "Community property," she snapped irritably.

Fortunately the airport limo arrived at that moment, and Kathleen and Mel boarded with half a dozen other passengers going to the same hotel. Mel didn't sit next to Kathleen. Instead he sat across the aisle, making conversation with an attractive redhead.

He's probably trying to make a date with her, Kathleen thought ruefully.

She rode to the hotel in stony silence, angrier at herself for feeling so jealous than she was at him for flirting so openly. If I didn't care, nothing he does would bother me, she told herself.

I wish it didn't bother me.

* * *

"Looks like we're not only staying in the same hotel but on the same floor," Mel chided her gently as they rode up in the elevator together.

"Almost as if you planned it that way," she said coldly, not bothering to look at him.

"Me?" He laughed aloud. "Not a chance, sweetheart." He turned to the bellhop carrying his bags. "Got a good restaurant in the hotel?"

"More than one," the younger man assured him, naming them according to quality. And price, Mel suspected. With the most expensive at the top of the list, no doubt.

He turned to Kathleen again. "We're both alone in town, neither of us knows anyone else," he started. "Maybe we could have dinner together—"

"I don't think so," she said sharply as the door opened and she stepped out of the elevator. "I'm going to have room service."

He stood there, watching her walk down the hall.

"You two know each other?" the bellhop asked, making an attempt at conversation.

Mel thought about it for a moment. "Sometimes I wonder," he admitted.

"He *knew!*" Kathleen spit. "He *knew*—that's why he gave it up without a fight!"

The opened suitcase lying on the bed was definitely not hers. It was filled with things like jeans, shirts, socks, underwear—and a shaving kit.

It was Mel's suitcase. And he knew it!

Furious, she closed the suitcase and zipped it up. It's about time I gave my ex-husband a piece of my mind, she thought as she left her room, suitcase in hand, and headed down the hall to find his room. Of course, it wouldn't do to tell him she was going to give him a piece of her mind. He'd only make some dumb remark like, "Not too big a piece, sweetheart—you don't have it to spare."

Then she'd have to kill him.

She knocked on the door forcefully, hoping she had the right room. If she hadn't been so angry, she would have been relieved to see him open the door.

"Change your mind about dinner?" he asked cheerfully.

"Fat chance. You have something that belongs to me," she informed him as she shoved the suitcase at him. "And I believe this is yours."

"I thought you knew your own suitcase when you saw it," he chided her.

"And you knew it was yours!" she shot back at him. "What did you hope to find in my suitcase, anyway?"

Now he wasn't smiling. "There's nothing in there I need," he said, giving her the other suitcase.

"Not even my notes?"

His eyes met hers. "I never needed your notes to make it before," he said coldly. "Why would I need them now?"

Kathleen opened her mouth to say something, then changed her mind. No, she told herself, he's not going to get to me. I won't let him.

She grabbed her suitcase. "You need something," she said evenly, "but I'm not sure what it could be." Then she turned and walked out the door, slamming it in her wake.

Kathleen reprimanded herself over a room service dinner of salad and fresh fruit. She shouldn't have blown up like that, shouldn't have accused him of having ulterior motives in taking her suitcase. He never needed her notes. He never needed her.

Maybe that was the problem all along. Maybe things would have been different if she had felt he needed her, if she'd ever felt they were on an equal footing. But it hadn't been that way. He'd always been so self-sufficient, both professionally and personally. His career had taken off like a heat-seeking missile while her own had progressed at a snail's pace.

Ego, in the end, had been responsible for the failure of their marriage.

My ego, that is, she thought miserably.

Mel, not crazy about the idea of sitting in a restaurant alone while everyone else was paired up like the passengers on Noah's Ark, had settled on a room service meal himself—pizza, egg rolls and beer. He parked the cart beside the bed, kicked off his shoes and took off his shirt, then stretched out on his bed to watch a movie on pay-TV while he ate.

He couldn't figure Kathleen out. She'd been defensive in varying degrees since the divorce, but she'd never accused him of anything underhanded. She'd always known better. Even when she was angriest, the rational part of her had known he'd never had to resort to anything unethical to get his story.

Her unexpected accusations had infuriated him. But the unanswered question was, would it have angered him as much if it had come from someone else?

The next morning, Kathleen was up early. Over a light breakfast of juice and a croissant, she went over her list of possible contacts and looked up numbers in the telephone directory. Some weren't listed. She called directory assistance and was told the numbers were unlisted.

"Well, that reduces the prospects considerably," she said aloud, drawing in a deep breath. She studied the list for a long moment, considering her options.

"It's something, anyway."

Mel had just finished a huge breakfast of eggs, bacon, potatoes, biscuits and juice. "Time to get to work," he told himself, polishing off the remaining crumbs on his plate. He took a small black notebook from the pocket inside his leather jacket and flipped through the pages until he found what he was looking for, then went to the phone and dialed. "Dave? Mel Riggs here," he identified himself. "Yeah, it has been a long time. Five years now, isn't it?" He laughed. "Listen, I need a favor...."

Kathleen went to the brokerage firm where Rollins had once been a partner. Everyone there refused to talk to her except Rollins's former secretary. "The firm has washed its collective hands of him," the older woman explained. "They feel his situation is bad for business."

"The official company line?" Kathleen asked.

The woman nodded. "You could say that, yes," she conceded.

"And how do you feel about it?" Kathleen wanted to know.

She shrugged. "It doesn't matter what I think," she said simply.

"It matters to me."

The woman hesitated. "I think he was desperate," was all she would say.

Mel was across town interviewing the Rollins's eldest son, a high-level executive with an independent oil company.

"Nice view you've got here," Mel observed, taking in the view from Rollins's sixteenth-floor office in downtown Dallas.

"Thank you." Rollins Junior didn't bother to hide his impatience. "You haven't told me, Mr. Riggs. What brings you here?"

"I want to talk to you about your father."

The other man shook his head. "I have nothing to say about my father—to you or anyone else," he said firmly.

Mel smiled, undaunted. I've got my work cut out for me, he thought.

Kathleen returned to the hotel that evening feeling as though she'd spent the day in a war zone. She'd lost track of how many doors had been slammed in her face, how many phones had been hung up on her in the past few days. I'm getting nowhere fast, she thought dismally.

But she wasn't ready to give up, throw in the towel. Not by a long shot.

She saw Mel waiting for the elevator as she crossed the lobby. "Great," she groaned under her breath. "Just what I *don't* need to top off a perfectly dreadful day."

She would have avoided him if there had been another way to get to her room, but she just wasn't up to climbing fourteen flights of stairs—especially after the day she'd had. Drawing in a deep breath, she headed for the elevator, fully prepared to ignore him.

Trouble was, he ignored her first.

That infuriated her, though she wasn't quite sure why. Wasn't that what she wanted, to not have to talk to him, to not have to put up with his sharp tongue? So why, now that he was keeping his mouth shut—definitely a first—did it make her so angry?

Glancing at him out of the corner of her eye as they rode up to the fourteenth floor alone and in total silence, she felt dangerously near the boiling point. Look at him, she thought. He looks so smug.

And he was looking at her, thinking: There's that haughty air of hers again. Jeez, I hate it when she acts like that.

She looked away. Act like you don't know he's alive.

She wants me to think she doesn't even know I'm alive, he thought, trying hard not to smile.

What did I ever see in him?
What did I ever see in her?

It was the morning of her last day in Dallas. Kathleen was having breakfast in the hotel restaurant, which offered an all-you-can-eat buffet featuring every culinary temptation imaginable. Kathleen had taken only fruit, juice and a bagel. She sat alone at a table in the crowded restaurant, going over her notes as she ate. Until her waitress interrupted her.

"Excuse me," she said, somewhat hesitantly. "The restaurant is full, and we have people waiting. Would you mind sharing your table?"

Kathleen looked up and smiled. "Of course not," she said pleasantly. It would be a welcome change to have someone to talk to about something other than the Rollins case, she thought.

The waitress was returning. "Right here, sir," she said, gesturing toward Kathleen's table.

Kathleen looked up, and her mouth fell open. "I don't believe this," she half groaned as Mel seated himself across from her.

He looked at her, and he wasn't smiling. "That makes two of us," he said quietly.

"You didn't ask for this?" Her tone was disbelieving.

He was almost scowling. "Hardly," he said. "In fact, I think I'll ask to be moved to another table."

He started to signal their waitress, but Kathleen raised a hand to stop him. "Don't bother," she told him. "I'm almost finished. I'll be leaving soon."

"Don't leave on my account," he responded in a cool tone.

"Not a chance," she assured him. "I have to pack before checkout time."

He raised an eyebrow. "You're leaving?"

She nodded. "I've done all I can here," she said with a sigh of resignation. "No point in sticking around."

"I'll be here a few more days," he told her. "I've got more interviews lined up."

Now why doesn't that surprise me? she wondered as he sauntered off to the buffet, plate in hand. He'd always had a knack for getting into places where no one else could go, gaining access to people no one else could get to.

He returned to their table a few minutes later, his plate heaped with eggs, bacon, pancakes, sausage and biscuits. "Some things never change," Kathleen observed. "I can remember when that was just an appetizer for you."

He took a bite. "I may go back—at least once," he admitted.

"And you never gain an ounce." Kathleen pointed out the unfairness of their physical differences.

"Metabolism," he offered in explanation.

"Right," she said in a disbelieving tone.

She didn't leave right away, as she'd intended. She stayed as long as she could, keeping one eye on her watch. For once she wished she didn't have to run. This was, without a doubt, the most pleasant conversation they'd had in a long time.

How long would it be before it happened again? It made her think of Halley's comet. . . .

The flight back to Saint Louis was uneventful. The weather was good, and the plane had encountered only very mild turbulence. When she arrived at Lambert Field, there had been only a short wait for her luggage, and the shuttle to the Park'n Fly lot was waiting when she went outside.

Now, as she drove home—in surprisingly light traffic—she found herself thinking, not about the book or what she had or hadn't accomplished in Dallas, but about the encounter with Mel over breakfast that morning. Unbelievably pleasant, she thought. For once, it didn't feel like an armed truce.

There were times he reminded her of a wicked little boy, too bright and too inventive for his own good, who just couldn't resist getting into trouble. That little boy had been one of the most endearing facets of Mel's personality. It brought out all of my maternal instincts, she recalled now. It had been a long time since that mischievous little boy had surfaced, but he was very much in evidence this morning in Dallas.

If only he'd stuck around, Kathleen thought wistfully.

During the day, Mel was far too busy to think about anyone or anything but the book and the research he was doing. He barely managed to take time for breakfast or lunch—most of the time those meals were eaten on the run. But at night, it was a different story.

At night he thought about Kathleen. Alone in that hotel room, too wired to sleep but too exhausted to work, he would lie awake and think.

You're such an idiot, he thought. How can you still be so hung up on a woman who walked out on you? How can you feel anything for any woman after having had it done to you twice?

Twice. It had been twice. The first woman to walk out on him was his mother, and that event had had more impact on his life than any other.

Until his marriage to Kathleen fell apart.

She'd never known how deeply the divorce had hurt him. He was good at hiding his feelings. Maybe a little too good, he thought. Wasn't that one of her biggest complaints against him? That he hid behind a sharp wit, never giving too much or seeming to take anything too seriously?

If only she knew why, he thought, before he drifted off into a dream . . .

"Oh, Mel. . . ."

"Kathy . . . Kathy . . ."

She was there in his room, in his bed. In his arms. And their lovemaking was just as good as it had ever been. The smell of her perfume . . . the softness of her skin . . . the lushness of her breasts . . . the taste of her lips . . . the fresh, clean scent of her hair. . . . Nobody had ever affected him the way she did. He'd never wanted another woman—any other woman—the way he wanted her.

"It's been so long, Kathy," he whispered, kissing her hair.

Her hands moved over his bare shoulders, down his back. "Too long," she agreed. "Much too long."

"I've missed you, babe."

"I love you, Mel," she told him then. "I've always loved you."

Before he could respond, he woke up.

"I have a feeling he accomplished a lot more than I did," Kathleen confided to Darcy over lunch. "He has contacts you wouldn't believe. I don't think there's anyone he can't gain access to."

"You have contacts," Darcy pointed out.

"Not like his," Kathleen admitted, even though she hated to do so, even to Darcy. "Sometimes I think he's got connections to everybody on the face of the planet."

"Do I detect some feelings of discouragement there?" Darcy wanted to know.

"I have my days."

"I get the feeling there's a little more to it than that," Darcy pressed.

Kathleen hesitated for a moment. "Well, yes—there is," she said finally. "I had breakfast with Mel the morning I left Dallas. It wasn't planned or anything like that. The hotel restaurant was crowded, and I was asked if I'd be willing to share my table." She gave a little laugh. "If I'd known they were going to put my ex-husband at my table, I probably would have said no.''

"So what happened?''

"I was surprised. It was the most pleasant encounter we've had since the divorce.''

"Then what's bothering you?'' Darcy asked, puzzled.

"That *is* what's bothering me.''

Mel did *not* have a quiet, uneventful flight back to Saint Louis. In fact, it was anything but uneventful. The plane hit turbulence just out of Love Field, and the Fasten Seat Belt sign remained on throughout the rest of the flight. Over southern Missouri they ran into a thunderstorm.

Several times the pilot's voice came over the PA to update the passengers on the existing weather conditions. There was a possibility of a landing at an airport other than Saint Louis. Some of the passengers were anxious but trying to hide it. Others were visibly upset. Mel, a seasoned traveler who'd experienced just about everything, was calm.

At first.

Conditions got progressively worse. The plane seemed to bounce about wildly in the dark, turbulent sky. Twice, lightning narrowly missed hitting the plane. Two women across the aisle were near hysteria. The man sitting in front of Mel was looking out the window anxiously. On the surface, Mel remained calm, but inside he was as worried as anyone else on that plane. He'd experienced turbulence before—but never anything like this.

And in the back of his mind he saw, not his life flashing by like a movie in fast forward, but what he could be missing if the plane were to crash, if his life were to end tonight. It came as a complete surprise to him that the uppermost thought in his mind was what could have been between him and Kathleen.

I still love her, he thought. I must have rocks in my head, but God help me, I still love her.

He wondered what things would have been like if they had stayed together. He wondered what it would have been like if they could have gotten back together. He wondered if they'd ever have another chance to try....

The plane lurched, making a sudden drop in altitude. This is it, Mel thought, admitting his fear only to himself. We're not going to make it. I'm going to die without having another chance to tell her I love her.

"Ladies and gentlemen, this is Captain McAndrews...try to land in Saint Louis...please secure all loose objects...remove eyeglasses..."

Mel was only half listening to the pilot's voice as the plane began a shaky descent to Lambert Field. He'd been in some precarious positions before, but this was the closest he'd ever been to death. He looked out the window again. Lightning flashed continually, the only light in an eerily black sky. The plane seemed to be moving too fast, plummeting toward the earth. His heart thudded wildly in his chest, racing every bit as fast as the 727. Mel closed his eyes.

It'll all be over soon.

Then, a few moments later, he felt a thud as the plane came down on the runway, rolling to a bumpy stop at the gate.

When Mel opened his eyes, he realized he'd broken out in a cold sweat.

Seven

"**D**isaster was narrowly averted...flight arriving in Saint Louis from Dallas...727 flying in during the electrical storm...safe landing at Lambert...."

Kathleen was only dimly aware of the TV newscaster's voice as she revised the chapter she'd completed that day—and it never occurred to her that it could have been the flight Mel was on. She wasn't even sure exactly when he was coming home, so she had no idea that her ex-husband—the man she still loved—could have been killed.

Her mind was on the interview she'd scheduled for the next day. Tomorrow morning she had an appointment with J. L. Preston, the defense attorney handling the Rollins case. Preston had been surprisingly willing to talk to her. Or maybe it was not so surprising, now that she thought about it. Preston hated the idea of Washburn doing a book on the case. He was now in the process of trying to have Washburn removed from the case. "Conflict of interest," he'd called it.

In fact, a lot of people had been screaming "conflict of interest" lately. In Washburn's case, she understood it. He was prosecuting the case. He shouldn't be allowed to profit from his book until the case was over. But Mel was another story. He was a reporter. It had been his job to write about the case for the paper. How could it possibly be considered a conflict of interest for him to write a book about it?

Kathleen smiled, thinking about her scheduled meeting with Preston. It should be interesting.

These near-death experiences are nothing to mess with.

Mel thought about it as he drove home from the airport, for the first time in his life keeping within the posted speed limits. He'd almost left the car at the Park'n Fly and taken a cab home. He was still shaking. He'd probably shake at the thought of that flight for the next six months.

Or longer, he thought.

Traffic was light on the interstate, and he was grateful for that. Though the drive from the airport to his place seemed to take forever, he was actually home in less than half an hour.

From the moment the 727 had landed safely, he'd been telling himself he was going to call Kathleen the minute he got home, that he wasn't going to wait even a minute longer to tell her what a fool he'd been, how much he still loved her and wanted to try again to make their relationship work—if she'd have him. But now that he was home, he found he was so wiped out—physically exhausted and mentally drained—that he barely had the energy for a quick shower before he fell into bed. It's late, he told himself. She'd probably be in bed by now. And even if he did call her now, he'd probably sound like a blubbering idiot, and she wouldn't take him seriously.

I'll call her in the morning, he promised himself.

"And that's Rod Stewart with 'Downtown Train' at nine-twenty this Friday morning," the disk jockey's voice crackled over the car radio. "Coming up, we've got Linda Ronstadt and Aaron Neville, Lou Gramm, and Madonna."

Kathleen stifled a yawn. For some reason, she hadn't slept well last night. She'd stayed up late—well past midnight, which was late for her—working on the book, and when she finally did get to bed, she was too tense to sleep.

But it wasn't the book that had been on her mind. It was Mel.

She'd been thinking about him a lot, about that last morning in Dallas—a painful reminder of what they'd once shared. It seems like another lifetime, she thought, like it happened to someone else.

She wondered if he was still in Dallas. He'd said he was staying on for a few days. That was on Tuesday.

Maybe I'll give him a call, she thought.

"This is Kathleen. I'm sorry I'm not able to take your call right now, but that's life in the rat race. If you'll leave your name and number and a brief message at the beep, I'll get back to you just as soon as I can. Thanks for calling."

At the sound of the tone on the other end of the line, Mel hung up without bothering to leave a message. He didn't want to talk to some stupid answering machine; he wanted to talk to Kathleen.

He had so much to tell her. But how would she respond? Would she take him seriously? Would it make any difference? Would it matter to her at all, knowing he still cared? Or was it too late?

No, leaving a message wouldn't do. Not this time. He had to talk to her face-to-face. But maybe...

He snatched up the phone and dialed again, drumming his fingers impatiently on the desk top as the answering machine's outgoing message played out. At the sound of the beep, he started talking. "Hi, Kathy. Mel. I'm back in town, and I'd really like to talk to you." He paused. "Give me a call, okay?"

He hung up slowly, drawing in a deep breath. Okay, Kathy, he thought. The ball's in your court— for now.

"Frankly, I was surprised you were willing to talk to me at all," Kathleen admitted, sitting across the desk from J. L. Preston, a man considered to be one of the best criminal defense attorneys in the country—the equal of the likes of Melvin Belli and F. Lee Bailey. He certainly is one of the most expensive, Kathleen thought wryly. But he certainly didn't look the part. He was short, myopic, and always looked in desperate need of a barber and a good tailor—but behind the disheveled exterior was one of the shrewdest legal minds in the country.

"Why should you be surprised?" he asked pleasantly. "It seems to me you would have expected my cooperation.

"You mean because I'm competing with C. W. Washburn," Kathleen concluded, smiling.

"It doesn't hurt that you're also Mel Riggs's ex-wife."

"You've done your homework," Kathleen said. "I'm impressed."

"It stands to reason you must feel the same way I do about their joint project," Preston went on.

"I see." Kathleen wasn't about to explain to Preston or anyone else her relationship with Mel. Especially since she couldn't even explain it to herself.

"Just what did you think you were doing?" Washburn demanded angrily.

Mel looked unconcerned. "It's called research, C.W.," he answered calmly. "All writers do it."

"You're not doing a story for the newspaper now, Melvin," Washburn reminded him. "And you're not working alone on this one. Where do you get off, flying to Dallas without even discussing it with me?"

"Listen, *Mr.* Washburn," Mel began evenly, "you're not a writer. You're a lawyer. A prosecutor. I'm a writer. That's why you took me on as a collaborator, remember?''

"Get to the point, Riggs," Washburn said testily.

"I know what I'm doing. I've been doing it for a long time, and at the risk of sounding arrogant, I'm good at it. You want this book to be the first one in the stores? Then don't slow me down with a lot of stupid restrictions.''

"Now just a minute—'' Washburn began.

Mel's eyes met the prosecutor's. "Tie my hands and all bets are off," he said with finality.

"It's been interesting, Mr. Preston," Kathleen said as she stood up and reached across the desk to shake the lawyer's hand.

"Happy to have been of assistance," he said pleasantly. "If there's anything further I can do, let me know.''

She hesitated momentarily. "Actually, there is one more thing," she said finally. "I'd like to talk to your client.''

Preston's smile vanished. "I'm afraid that's not possible.''

"I need to interview Rollins himself," Mel told Washburn.

The prosecutor laughed aloud at the thought—something he didn't do very often. "You must be kidding. Preston will never let you near him."

"I've got to interview him," Mel maintained stubbornly. "I just have to find a way to convince Preston it's in his client's best interest."

"If you manage that, you'd better get out of the newspaper business and get into politics," Preston said skeptically. "It'll take an exceptional negotiator to convince Preston of that."

Mel looked at him. "It might be easier if everyone in the English-speaking world didn't know I'm your collaborator."

But when Mel left Washburn's office, he wasn't thinking about how he was going to talk Preston into letting him interview Rollins.

He was thinking about Kathleen.

Traffic on eastbound Highway 40 was bumper-to-bumper. Kathleen sat in her car, in a seemingly endless sea of cars, half listening to the radio as she inched along in the traffic. She was thinking about her meeting with Preston. He'd been unbelievably cooperative, willing to accommodate her in any way.

Until she asked to see Rollins.

Why had he never allowed his client to be interviewed? It was a rule to which there had never been an exception, from the moment the man was arrested. Why? Kathleen wondered.

She turned her attention back to the radio. Cher was singing "If I Could Turn Back Time." Indeed, Kathleen thought, humming along. If I could turn back time. . . .

They'd been newlyweds and had been invited to a Halloween costume party. Mel had insisted they do something as a couple. Kathleen had suggested—only as a joke—that they go as Sonny and Cher, but he'd loved the idea.

"Do you really want to do this?" she had asked.

"Sure," Mel said with a wicked grin. "It'll be fun. Wait and see."

"I have a feeling I'm going to regret this," she said, positioning herself in front of the mirror as she struggled to tuck all of her hair under a long, black wig. "I don't have the body for this costume. This stuff's for skinny gals."

"Hey—at least you've got curves to show off," he pointed out.

"I'm not Cher, that's for sure," she said.

He came over to plant a kiss on her cheek. "Well, I, for one, am glad," he assured her.

Kathleen's thoughts returned to the present. He'd loved her the way she was. At least he had then—

before everything started to go wrong between them.

When love was no longer enough, she thought.

I wonder if she got my message yet.

Mel was thinking about it as he let himself into his apartment, loaded down with heavy grocery bags. He did serious grocery shopping at least once a month, whether he needed to or not—and most of the time he didn't, since he usually ate out and often at fast-food restaurants. Kathleen had once said—more than once, actually—that food didn't taste good to him unless it was wrapped in paper or came in a cardboard box. Sometimes, he conceded to himself as he started taking everything out of the bags, I think she might be right. Let's see . . . lunch meat, chips, dip, frozen dinners, cupcakes, canned soup. Yep, I guess she's right.

He smiled to himself, remembering the first time he and Kathleen had gone grocery shopping together. . . .

"You really want to buy that?" Kathleen had asked, making a face at the sight of the huge bag of candy Mel was about to toss into their shopping cart.

"Sure," he said cheerfully. "Why not?"

"It's junk. All you get from eating that stuff is a lot of empty calories."

"And a heck of a sugar rush," he maintained. "Sort of like sex—the pleasure it gives is the main draw."

She gave him a knowing smile. "Oh, really?"

"You bet. And when we get home, I'll prove it."

That night, they indulged in a little of one and a lot of the other. That night, and a lot of other nights afterward.

His thoughts returned to the present abruptly as he realized the red light on his answering machine was flashing. He pressed the button to replay the messages, listening as he put the groceries away. Nothing important, he thought as the last message played. I wonder if Kathy got my message yet?

She had.

She was listening to her messages at almost the same time he'd been checking his. She didn't have many. Carla had called—to discuss business, no doubt. Darcy had also called—her husband was making one of his rare appearances on the home front, so she had to cancel plans to meet Kathleen for dinner that evening. It's just as well, Kathleen thought. I should be staying home anyway. I should be working on the book.

The next message was from Mel. Oh—so he is back, she thought as she listened to the message. In spite of the pleasantness of their last encounter, she was surprised that he wanted to see her.

She picked up the phone and started to dial. She couldn't wait to find out what it was all about.

Mel was making himself a sandwich when the phone rang. He picked up the wall phone in the kitchen, continuing the careful construction of his sandwich.

"Yeah?"

"Mel, it's Kathleen. I got your message. What's up?"

"I think we need to talk."

"You said that on the tape. About what?"

"I'd rather not discuss it on the phone," he insisted, going to the refrigerator for a jar of mayonnaise.

"Sounds cryptic." There was a pause on the other end. "Okay, then. When?"

He looked at his watch. "How about tonight?"

"Where and what time?" she wanted to know.

"McGurk's, around nine?" he suggested.

Kathleen laughed. "Nobody goes to McGurk's to talk!" The pub was known for its Irish musicians, generally considered the best this side of Dublin.

"All right—you choose the place, then."

"The Cheshire Inn. Breakfast, tomorrow morning," she suggested off the top of her head.

He paused. "Tomorrow?" He was a little disappointed but tried not to show it. "Well, all right."

"What time's good for you?" she asked.

"Eight-thirty, nine?"

"Let's make it nine."

"Fine."

"See you then."

The receiver clicked in his ear. He hung up and went back to the monster sandwich he'd created.

She doesn't seem all that anxious to see me, he thought.

"When did you get back?" Kathleen asked over breakfast.

"Thursday evening." He looked around, not at all surprised that she'd picked this restaurant. It was her kind of place. It looked like a Tudor mansion, inside and out—right down to the suit of armor on display near the entrance.

She took a bite of her grapefruit. "How was your flight?" she asked, her tone deceptively casual.

"Like a bad movie." He took a forkful of scrambled eggs. "We had to land during an electrical storm—and I wasn't at all sure I was going to be walking away from it."

Then she remembered what she'd seen on TV that night. "That was your plane?" she asked. "I mean, you were on *that* flight?"

He nodded. For once, he wasn't smiling. "I'll tell you, there's nothing like being in a plane going down to make you take stock of your life," he confided.

"It was that bad?" she asked, putting her fork down abruptly.

"From where I sat, yeah." His expression was grim.

She sat silent for a long moment, stunned by the thought that, but for the grace of God, he could have been killed. The thought made her physically ill, but she was struggling not to let it show.

"What did you want to talk to me about?" she finally managed.

His eyes met hers. "Us," he said quietly. "I wanted to talk about us."

Eight

"Us?" Kathleen wasn't quite sure she understood.

"I'd been thinking about this before," he said quickly, "while I was in Dallas. I realized my feelings for you were still deep when you alluded to my lack of professional ethics. It hurt more than it angered me. I realized you couldn't hurt me if I didn't still care."

Kathleen said nothing. She was thinking about what Carla had said: Love doesn't hurt when it goes away. It only hurts while it's still around.

"I know a lot of time has passed, that there's a lot of bad blood between us," Mel was saying, "but there's still a lot of feeling, too—at least on my part."

"Mine, too," Kathleen admitted somewhat hesitantly, avoiding his eyes by fixing her gaze on her plate, "but feeling, as you call it, has never been enough for us, Mel. *Love* has never been enough."

"How do you figure?"

"We loved each other then," she reminded him. "I think we loved each other about as much as either of us is capable of loving anyone—but it wasn't enough to keep us together. It wasn't enough to get us through the rough times. It wasn't enough to get us through our so-called differences of opinion."

He shook his head. "I feel like such a fool," he said with a weak laugh. "I came here with this nifty little speech prepared—rehearsed it half a dozen times in my head on the way over here—how being faced with my own mortality made me see how wrong I've been, how wrong it was for us to split up. I was going to tell you—ah, what the heck? It doesn't matter now." Throwing his napkin down, he got to his feet so abruptly that the table shook in his wake. He yanked a twenty-dollar bill from his pocket and threw it down in front of her. "My mistake."

"Mel—" she began.

But he wouldn't listen. He turned and walked out without even a backward glance.

I blew it, she told herself as she drove home.

She'd left the restaurant right after he walked out on her. There had been no point in staying when she no longer had any appetite, was there? He hadn't given her a chance to finish what she'd been trying to tell him.

He didn't give me a chance to tell him I still love him, too.

If Mel could have horsewhipped himself, he would have. How could he have been so stupid? What had made him think that, after all these years, she would even consider taking him back?

He should have known it wouldn't be that easy.

It's not that easy. He should have known that.

It made her more than a little angry. What made him think he could suddenly decide he wants me back in my life and I'd be sitting around, just waiting for him?

The answer was simple. *He knows I still love him.*

* * *

She must know I still love her, he thought, frustrated.

He'd handled it badly with her. After all that had gone wrong between them, how could he have expected her to just rush back into his arms?

She must have thought I was one arrogant jerk.

He hadn't changed. He was still an arrogant jerk. So why was she so miserable? she wondered. Why was she so upset that he'd walked out on her— again? Why did it bother her so much that she hadn't had the chance to finish what she'd been trying to tell him?

Why, she asked herself, do I still love him?

Why did he still love her? It was a mystery to him. She was just like his mother. Her career, her ambitions were the most important things in her life. Nothing, no one else mattered, only her pursuit of success. When forced to choose, she'd chosen her work—just as his mother had done.

Women, Mel thought. They're all alike.

Men, Kathleen thought. They're all alike.

Most men didn't want their women to have careers. They wanted them at home, cooking, sewing, making babies, and watching soap operas.

I'll show him, she thought angrily.

I'll show her, he thought bitterly.

He didn't need her or any other woman. He never had and never would. He'd learned not to depend on a woman—for the fulfillment of any of his needs—at an early age. It was a lesson he'd never forgotten.

She's never going to change, he thought with certainty.

"He's never going to change," Kathleen told Darcy.

"Obviously that's not true," Darcy said reasonably. "You just said he wanted to see you because he'd realized he still loved you and wanted to try again."

"Sure he did," Kathleen said with a nod. "He thought he could wake up one morning and decide he still loved me and wanted me back, and in spite of the divorce, in spite of all the years that have passed, in spite of everything that went wrong between us, I'd just go rushing back into his arms as though nothing had happened."

"You mean you wouldn't?" Darcy looked unconvinced.

"No, I *wouldn't,*" she insisted. "I have my pride."

"Maybe," Darcy started slowly, "but your pride won't keep you warm at night. It won't give you any comfort when the rest of the world's giving you a raw deal. And it won't make love to you."

Kathleen's laugh was hollow. "Is that all you ever think about?" she wanted to know.

"Yes," Darcy admitted without hesitation, "especially when my husband is out of town. Which, unfortunately, is most of the time. Are you saying you *don't* want Mel back?" she asked in her typically direct manner.

"No—I'm saying I haven't been sitting around all these years waiting for him to come to his senses," Kathleen said stubbornly. "I was trying to explain that, while I still loved him and wanted more than anything to try again, I was concerned that too much had gone wrong between us, that I couldn't just rush into this. That I had to take it slowly."

"And?"

"I never got the chance to tell him," she said. "It wasn't what he wanted to hear, so he wouldn't listen."

"She wouldn't listen," Mel told Richard. "Her mind was already made up, so she just shut me out."

"Frankly, I'm surprised you even tried," Richard admitted. "I didn't think you wanted any part of a reconciliation—now or at any other time."

"Neither did I." Mel frowned. "I guess I even surprise myself sometimes."

"Consider yourself lucky she didn't take you back," Richard advised. "Take it from the voice of experience—you're better off."

"Yeah—I guess you're right," Mel conceded, stopping to buy a hot dog from a vendor outside the Municipal Courts building.

"Sure, I'm right." Richard headed up the steps toward the main entrance, on his way to sit in on a trial he'd been writing about in his column. "You'll see."

"Yeah." Mel took a bite of his hot dog as he shifted his gaze to the busy downtown traffic. "I've been telling myself the same thing all along. So why don't I believe it?"

Kathleen stared at the computer screen until her eyes couldn't take it anymore. Then she leaned back in her chair and rubbed her eyes in an attempt to relieve the burning sensation.

She'd read somewhere—she didn't remember exactly where or when, only that it had been a long time ago—that no one became a writer if they were capable of doing anything else. She was beginning to believe it was true. In spite of her years of experience as a writer, as a reporter, she had not been prepared for the demands of writing a book.

This was anything but easy.

She decided she needed a break and went into the kitchen for some tea. No, it's definitely not easy, she admitted to herself, but it is what I've always wanted.

What she was no longer sure of was exactly *why* she wanted it. In the beginning, she wanted it for herself. She'd wanted to prove herself. She'd wanted recognition, the thrill of seeing her name on a book cover—and hopefully on the bestseller lists, too. In the beginning, that would have been enough. More than enough. But now...

Now there was Mel. Mel, who had never really accepted her ambitions. Mel, who'd tried every way he could to discourage her. Mel, who always told her she'd never make it in the so-called big leagues. From the day they admitted their marriage was over, proving herself to him had become more important to her than realizing her goals for her own satisfaction.

It didn't take much guesswork to figure out why.

Not bad. Not bad at all.

A satisfied smile came to Mel's lips as he reviewed the most recently completed chapter on the computer screen. It had turned out much better than he'd expected. The trip to Dallas had definitely been worthwhile.

Dallas.

He frowned. Thinking about Dallas made him think about Kathleen. And thinking about Kathleen was something he didn't want to do. Especially not now when things were going so well. Working with the likes of C. W. Washburn had never been his idea of a collaboration made in heaven, and he swore, even now, that he'd never collaborate again—he was a writer who *needed* to work alone—but, by golly, it *was* working.

The last thing he needed right now was to be distracted by thoughts of his ex-wife.

The woman he still loved.

God help me, I do still love her, he thought miserably. I must be out of my mind, but I do.

Some people never learn.

I shouldn't have let him walk out on me, Kathleen thought, mentally kicking herself. I should have stopped him, made him hear me out.

That was a laugh. As if she could really have stopped him. Nobody stopped Melvin Riggs from doing anything, once he'd made up his mind. Stopping him from walking out of that restaurant would have been like trying to stop a raging bull.

Still, it was going to keep eating away at her until she did tell him how she felt, until he understood that, while she still loved him and wanted to give it another try every bit as much as he did, she had some serious concerns. Legitimate concerns.

She looked at her watch. Creature of habit that he was, she had a pretty good idea where he'd be right now. She thought about it for only a moment before reaching a decision. Putting on her coat, she grabbed her purse and headed for the door.

She was going to tell him how she felt—whether he wanted to hear it or not.

There wasn't a table to be had at McGurk's.

The Irish pub on the city's south side, in the part of town known as Soulard, was packed that night. Standing room only, Mel thought as he squeezed into the only spot available at the bar and signaled the bartender, who brought him a Guinness.

They all knew him well at McGurk's.

He thought about it as he polished off his drink and waved to the bartender for another. He hadn't realized how tired he was until he'd finally stopped working for the day. He probably should have just taken a hot shower and gone to bed, but for reasons he didn't even understand himself, he needed this even more.

He needed to not be alone with thoughts of Kathleen.

"He just left," the bartender told Kathleen.

"It's only ten o'clock," she pointed out, as if the man behind the bar weren't aware of it.

"He'd been here a couple of hours," the bartender recalled. "First time I can remember he came in and didn't look like he was enjoying himself much."

"Apparently," she muttered, speaking more to herself than she had been to the bartender.

"What?"

"Oh—nothing," she said distractedly, realizing he'd heard her. "Thank you."

She left the pub and went to her car. He'd been there, just as she'd known he would be. She knew him so well.

Yet there were times she felt as if she didn't know him at all.

I might as well have stayed home, Mel thought.

He didn't know how long he'd been driving. In fact, now that he thought about it, he wasn't even sure *where* he'd been since he left the pub. He'd just started driving, needing to think, needing to clear his head.

This situation with Kathleen brought back memories—memories he would have rather left buried. Memories of another time, another woman...another woman he'd loved, another woman who'd left him....

He remembered a little boy confused by the sight of his mother packing her suitcases.

Just hers.

"Where are you going, Mom?"

"I have to go away for a while," she said distractedly.

"Go away?" He didn't really understand. "Without Dad? Without me?"

"Yes, Melvin," she said with unmasked impatience in her voice. "There's nothing for you to worry about. You'll be fine here with your father."

He looked at her. "You're not coming back, are you?" he wanted to know.

She hesitated for a moment as though she'd been tempted to lie, but finally said, "No. You're old enough to know the truth. I'm not coming back. I'm not happy and haven't been for a long time."

"What about me?" The little boy was frightened.

"You'll be better off here with your father," she insisted, carrying her bags to the front door. "He'll be home very soon now—you'll be fine here until he comes."

He looked at her accusingly. "You don't love me," he concluded.

She sighed. "I do love you, Melvin," she told him, "but I'm not cut out to be a mother."

"But Mom—"

A taxicab pulled up in front of the house. The driver blew the horn. The woman knelt to embrace the little boy and kiss his forehead. "I do love you," she told him again. "One day, you'll understand."

He stood on the front porch, watching her get into the cab—but as it pulled away, he ran after it, sobbing wildly. "Don't go, Mom!" he wailed. "Please don't go!"

But the cab didn't stop. He stood there in the street, crying and waving, long after the cab was out of sight.

It was the last time he saw her.

Tears streamed down Mel's cheeks as he drove. That image was still as clear in his mind as it had been the day it happened. Painfully clear.

One day, you'll understand.

That was what she had said. Some consolation that had been for a small child whose mother was about to walk out on him. "Someday you'll understand," he said aloud, his voice filled with contempt. "Wrong, *Mother*—I didn't understand then and I don't understand now. What kind of woman just walks out on her own child?"

And then: "Never again. Never will you or Kathy or any other woman get the chance to do it to me again."

Nine

I give up.

After she left McGurk's, Kathleen tried to call Mel twice, sure he'd gone home. Both times, she'd gotten his answering machine. She didn't leave a message. He probably wouldn't call her back anyway.

There were some things about Mel she had never understood and probably never would. How could he be so self-assured, even aggressive on a professional level, yet so insecure in his relationship with his wife? For a time, she'd wondered if he had at some time been deeply hurt in a serious relationship, but she'd never been certain, since he rarely talked about his life before he knew her. He'd never mentioned any previous relationships and talked little about his family, other than his father. He didn't talk about his mother at all.

His problems with women must have started with his mother, she thought, frustrated.

"Ms. Wilder, this is J. L. Preston," the voice on the other end of the telephone line identified itself.

"Yes, Mr. Preston. What can I do for you?" she asked, trying to sound businesslike.

"I think it might be more appropriate to ask what I can do for you," he responded pleasantly. "I've reconsidered your request."

"Oh?"

"I've spoken with my client, and he's agreed to talk to you," Preston explained.

She couldn't believe it at first. "When?" she asked finally.

"My secretary will call you," he promised, "as soon as the arrangements have been made."

"All right." She paused. "What changed your mind?"

"It's really quite simple," he assured her. "My client has decided he wants his side of the story told."

"I see."

"You'll be notified in a day or so."

"Thank you." She hung up slowly. His client wanted his side of the story told. What he meant was his client would talk to her because he didn't feel he'd get a fair shake from Mel and Washburn. No matter, she thought. I'll take the interview any way I can get it.

Now, if she could just get Mel off her mind.

Mel had endured a long, sleepless night.

It was the first time in years he'd dreamed about his mother. It was the first time in years he'd allowed himself to dwell on the past for long, giving his mother more than a passing thought.

Probably more than she's given me in all the years since she left, he thought bitterly.

He got out of bed and stumbled into the bathroom, clad only in his briefs. He looked at himself in the mirror under the harsh fluorescent light and decided he looked terrible. His hair was a mess. He needed a shave. I need a ten-year sabbatical, he thought as he splashed cold water on his face. But right now I'd settle for about fourteen hours' sleep.

If only Kathleen hadn't come to Saint Louis. If only neither of them were doing a book. He could be getting on with his life now. He could be enjoying the carefree life of a reconfirmed bachelor. He wouldn't be dealing with all of these unresolved feelings for his ex-wife.

"So what changed his mind?" Darcy wanted to know.

Kathleen shrugged. "He said Rollins wants to be sure his side of the story will be told," she answered, "but I think their real concern is what Mel and Washburn might say in their book."

"I'm sure," Darcy said with a nod. Then, after a long pause, she asked, "Have you seen Mel?"

"No." Kathleen's mood changed abruptly. Just thinking about him put her in a black mood. "I'm probably the last person on the face of the earth he wants to see right now."

"That bad, huh?"

Kathleen sucked in a deep breath. "Could we please talk about something else?" she begged. "Right now the last thing I want to talk about—or think about, for that matter—is my ex-husband."

But she knew that whether she wanted to or not, she wouldn't stop thinking about him.

"Look—whether you like it or not, this book *is* going to be written and it *is* going to be published," Mel reminded J. L. Preston. "Don't you think it would be in your client's best interests to have his side of the story told?"

"Definitely," Preston said with an easy smile. "But not to you."

Mel gave him a quizzical look. "I beg your pardon?"

"Come now, Mr. Riggs—surely you don't expect me to believe for a moment that you and my esteemed colleague would be willing to treat my client fairly in your book," Preston said in a disbelieving tone.

Mel considered it for a moment, trying not to chuckle at the thought. "As fairly as possible—under the circumstances," he assured the lawyer. "He is, after all, on trial for the murder of his own wife."

"On trial, but not yet convicted," Preston pointed out.

"It's only a matter of time."

"That attitude, Mr. Riggs, is precisely why I've advised my client not to speak with you at all," Preston responded, his tone suddenly cold. "Now, if you don't mind, I'm a busy man—" He gestured toward the door.

"Yeah. I get the picture." Mel got to his feet. "But as I said, this book *will* be published—with or without the cooperation of you and your client."

As he was leaving, he overheard Preston's secretary talking to someone on the telephone. "Yes,

Ms. Wilder—Mr. Preston has arranged for you to see Mr. Rollins at two this afternoon.''

Mel stopped in his tracks, trying not to appear too obvious—but convinced he was failing miserably.

So—Preston was allowing Rollins to talk to *Kathleen*. It didn't take much in the way of imagination to figure out why.

Mel thought about it as he drove home. Preston hadn't agreed to let Rollins talk to Kathleen because he was overly impressed with her as a writer or because he felt she'd go out of her way to be fair to Rollins. No...he'd done it because he knew Mel and Washburn were going to rip Rollins apart. He probably figured she'd at least be more objective.

The lesser of two evils, Mel thought wryly.

"I didn't kill her."

If Kathleen hadn't been following the case so closely for so long, if she weren't familiar with all of the evidence the state had against him, she might have believed him. Henry Rollins didn't *look* like a killer. He didn't look like he could kill a gnat, much less his own wife.

He *did* look absolutely sincere.

"All of the evidence says you did," Kathleen reminded him. "How do you explain that?"

"I wish I *could* explain it," Rollins said with a heavy sigh. "All I can be certain of is that I didn't do it. What's really incriminated me is that I took that new insurance policy out on June six months before she died."

"Not to mention the fact that your business interests are shaky and have been for some time now," Kathleen said.

"I didn't kill her," he maintained.

"Why don't you tell me what happened?" Kathleen suggested then.

"It's been in all the papers."

"I'd like to hear it from your viewpoint," she said, unable to think of a better word for it.

He nodded, frowning. "June accompanied me on most of my business trips," he recalled. "We both wanted it that way. June's not—she wasn't, that is—the athletic type. So when I'd go out to jog every morning, June would always stay at the hotel. She'd take a shower, do her hair and makeup, that sort of thing. When I returned, we'd have breakfast together. Usually room service.

"That morning, she was still asleep when I left. I was gone just over an hour. When I came back, I found her in the bathroom, on the floor," he went on. "The shower was still running. She was naked. She was still wet. She wasn't breathing."

He's good, Kathleen was thinking. Real good. If she didn't know better, she would have felt sorry for him.

What would Mel do in my place?

"Seems Preston's reconsidered his position. He's letting Kathy Wilder talk to Rollins."

Mel was calling C. W. Washburn from a pay phone. "I overheard his secretary making the arrangements."

Washburn laughed. "I'm not surprised," he said. "Preston's always been concerned about how this case would be treated in my book."

"Our book," Mel corrected.

"Our book. Of course," Washburn said, clearly an afterthought. "Not that it makes any difference whether your ex-wife talks to him or not."

"Right." As Mel hung up, he realized it wasn't the idea that someone else had gotten to Rollins before he did that bugged him.

It was that the someone was Kathy.

The interview had gone smoothly. Unfortunately there hadn't been any surprises—Rollins had told the same story, almost verbatim, that he'd told in court and, before that, to the police at least half a dozen times following his arrest. It was almost as if he rehearsed it.

And that was why, no matter how convincing he was, she didn't believe him.

He's guilty as sin, she thought as she drove home. He could probably fool someone who didn't know about that big, fat insurance policy he'd taken out on her six months before her death.

The thought that suddenly came to her made her laugh. It was a good thing Mel couldn't afford life insurance when they were still married!

"I guess it's cheaper than getting a divorce," Mel told Richard as they entered the county courthouse.

"Only if you don't get caught," Richard reminded him.

This was the last day of the trial. All of the evidence had been presented and all of the witnesses heard, and now both the prosecution and defense would present closing arguments. Not that any surprises were expected.

But my future as an author depends on the outcome of this trial, Mel was thinking. Nobody will want to publish a book about a murder without a killer.

He knew only too well that, if Rollins were not found guilty, the book, *his* book, could—and probably would—be canceled. And so would hers, he thought as Kathleen crossed his path and en-

tered the courtroom with that good-looking courtroom artist from the *Mirror* at her side.

"The bum," he muttered irritably.

"What?" Richard asked.

Mel's head jerked up, realizing suddenly that
he'd said it aloud. "Nothing," he said quickly.
"Just talking to myself."

"You do that often?" Richard asked with a grin.

"Only when my ex-wife's around." His tone was
sullen.

Richard laughed. "Ex-wives can have that effect
on a guy," he said, obviously speaking from experience.

It wasn't until they took their seats that Mel realized they were sitting directly in front of Kathleen and the Tom Selleck clone. Great, he thought.
Just what I need.

Though he vowed not to, he found himself unable to keep from looking over his shoulder at them
from time to time. Is she seeing him? he wondered.

He thinks we're involved, Kathleen thought
smugly. She deliberately moved a little closer to
further convince him.

What does she see in him? he wondered.

I could do a lot worse, she thought.

He's good-looking, but so what? Mel thought.

It's his looks, Kathleen thought. Even Mel is insecure being compared to an exceptionally good-looking man.

He's not her type, Mel told himself.

He's really not my type, but Mel doesn't know that, Kathleen thought.

They look awfully chummy, Mel concluded.

We're just friends, but what the heck? Let him wonder! she thought gleefully.

Neither of them heard the closing arguments.

Mel was awakened at 6:00 a.m. by the ringing telephone. Still half-asleep, he groped around in the darkness until his hand found the receiver and brought it clumsily to his ear.

"Hello?"

"Mel, it's Rich," said the voice on the other end.

"Rich?" Mel grumbled. "Jeez, don't you ever sleep?"

"Only during the day," Richard assured him. "I thought you'd want to hear the news before today's edition hits the stands."

Mel sat up in bed, suddenly alert. "What news?"

"Apparently there was some monkey business involving the Rollins jury. Preston's moving for a mistrial."

Ten

"**Y**ou're going *where?*"

"I never heard of it, either," Kathleen told Darcy as she packed her overnight bag. "All I know is that it's some little one-horse town in southeastern Missouri—far enough away to make it foolish to even think about trying to make it in one day."

Darcy still didn't quite understand. "Okay," she said with an uncertain nod, "but *why* are you going?"

"To talk to a woman who served on the Rollins jury," Kathleen said, zipping the suitcase. "She went down there right after the trial was over. She was the one who turned in the guards for allowing outsiders access to the sequestered jury.''

"Ah, yes—the party at the Holiday Inn," Darcy remembered.

"That's the one," Kathleen said with a nod. "I called her last night—she said she'd talk to me if I could come down there. She's living with her mother, who's apparently too ill to be left alone right now."

"Think Mel will be going down there, too?" Darcy asked casually, munching on an apple.

"If he hasn't already," Kathleen said with certainty. "This accusation, if proven to be true, could change the entire course of the trial."

"You think a mistrial will be declared?" Darcy wanted to know.

"Hard to tell." Kathleen deposited the overnighter on the floor near the door. "The defense could move for a new trial."

"Why don't they give up?" Darcy wondered aloud. "He's guilty as sin."

"Do you really think so?" Kathleen asked, genuinely interested.

"Everyone does," Darcy maintained. "I think they'd be hard-pressed to find another unbiased jury." She paused. "Why do you ask?"

"Just curious." She was thinking of her own response to Henry Rollins when she'd seen him in jail. It would have been so easy to be taken in by him.

But Mel, she thought with certainty, wouldn't have been.

The town was so small it wasn't even on the map.

Mel hoped the directions he'd been given were accurate. He hoped he could follow them. He hoped the predicted rain didn't arrive before he reached his destination.

He had to talk to this woman. She'd leveled some pretty serious accusations. So serious they could dramatically alter the course of the trial.

And the book.

Just what I don't need, he thought. He'd been moving along at a steady pace—while Washburn provided most of the material, Mel *was* doing most of the writing. If a mistrial was declared, or a new trial called for, it could prove to be a major setback.

It could mean another six weeks of work. Six weeks he hadn't counted on.

He turned on his windshield wipers. It was starting to rain.

The rain had turned into a downpour.

No point in trying to go any farther tonight,

Kathleen thought, on the lookout for an exit ramp. She'd just find a motel and wait out the storm. One more day wouldn't matter.

She finally spotted an exit ramp and got off the highway. After what seemed like an endless drive down a long, deserted road with very poor visibility, she finally spotted a small, run-down motel.

Looks like a hangout for perverts and traveling salesmen, Kathleen thought wryly. She pulled up in front of the office and stopped the car. She'd brought an umbrella, but she had a feeling it wouldn't help in that downpour. Deciding to take her chances without it, she jumped out of the car and made a run for the office, not noticing the car that came to a stop behind hers.

As she entered the small, dimly lit office, she saw the manager, a small, unshaven, shabbily dressed man in his mid-fifties, talking on the telephone. Two other men, equally seedy-looking, were leaning against the desk, telling off-color jokes. Kathleen thought they looked more like caricatures than real, live people.

The manager ignored her and kept talking. She rang the bell. Still no response.

"Jesus—are you following me?"

She jerked around just as Mel came into the office and closed the door. "Since I got here first, it

would seem that you're following me," she pointed
out.

The manager, having ended his phone call, came
back to the desk. "Whaddya want?" he asked in a
tone that was anything but polite.

"I'd like a room, please," Kathleen responded.

"Me, too," Mel echoed, waving a hand from
where he stood behind Kathleen.

"Only got one room left," he told them.

"I'll take it," Mel said quickly.

Kathleen swung around, glaring at him. "I was
here first," she pointed out.

He shrugged. "What do you expect me to do—
sleep in my car?" he asked.

"Apparently that's what you expect me to do,"
she said coldly.

He seemed to be considering the dilemma momentarily. "Well . . . we *could* share the room," he
suggested.

She laughed aloud at the thought. "You've got
to be kidding!"

"Am I laughing?"

"For once, no—but you should be," she told
him. "That's the funniest thing you've said in a
long time."

"It looks like the only option open to us at the
moment," he reminded her.

"Not at all," she said coldly. "You could always leave."

"Yeah, right." He gave a little chuckle. "In this downpour? Give me a break!"

She hadn't heard a word he'd said. She was rummaging through her bag in search of her checkbook and credit cards. While she was searching, Mel produced his MasterCard and signed for the room. "C'mon, kiddo," he told her.

She gave him a quizzical look.

He grinned. "We've got to figure out the sleeping arrangements."

"I don't know why I ever agreed to this," Kathleen complained as they attempted to hang a sheet from the ceiling to serve as a divider down the center of the bed. "This is crazy. This is insane. This is never going to work."

"It worked in the movies." He stood in the middle of the bed, removing a framed print of some landscape or other that was undoubtedly sold by the dozen at the local discount store.

Kathleen looked skeptical. "You don't really think you can hang this heavy blanket from *that*, do you?" she asked.

He warily eyed the small nail protruding from the wall. "Probably not," he said, shaking his head.

"Any more bright ideas?" she wanted to know.

He thought about it for a moment. "Nope," he admitted. "How about you?"

"Just one," she said thoughtfully.

He waited for her to go on. When she didn't, he gestured impatiently. "Well, come on—out with it," he urged. "At this point I'm willing to try just about anything."

"I'll sleep in the bed and you can have the floor," she said promptly.

He grinned. "Gee, that's really magnanimous of you," he said, amused, "but I couldn't possibly accept. It wouldn't be fair of me—"

"You can have all the blankets but one," she offered, ignoring the fact that he was quite obviously making fun of her.

He opened the small closet, pointing up at the shelf. "Big of you, considering there are only two blankets," he told her.

She glared at him. "Okay—sleep in the chair, then," she said crossly.

"*I* paid for the room," Mel reminded her. "How come *you're* deciding who sleeps where?"

"All right, then," she snorted, exasperated. "*I'll* sleep in the chair. Is that better?"

"Much, thank you," he said with a mocking gleam in his eye. "And to show you I can be a generous guy, I'll make you the same offer you made me. You can have one of the blankets."

She made a face. "You're all heart."

He grinned. "Not all of me, honey—or have you forgotten?"

"I've tried," she assured him.

"Tried but never succeeded."

He looked so smug! Unable to take it a minute longer, she grabbed her pajamas and robe from her already-opened suitcase and stalked into the bathroom, slamming the door as a pointed reminder that she *didn't* want to be disturbed.

It was like sleeping—or trying to sleep, anyway—on a pile of rocks.

The chair was old, and most of its stuffing had apparently disintegrated with age. The hard metal springs poked at her back and behind as she twisted and turned as much as the narrow space between the chair's rigid arms would allow, trying in vain to achieve at least a small amount of comfort. She looked over at Mel, sprawled out in the bed, sleeping soundly.

Well, what's it going to be? Are you going to play masochist all night, or are you going to swallow your pride and get a good night's sleep?

Pride lost in a big way to a sore bottom and aching back. Clutching her own blanket, she eased out of the chair—her aching body would not move any faster—and crossed the room to the bed.

She settled down onto the bed beside him and covered herself with the blanket. I never knew a lumpy mattress could feel so good, she thought, starting to drift off almost as soon as she lay down.

"I wondered how long it would take."

Instantly she was wide awake. "You rat!" she sputtered, furious. "You were awake all the time!"

He laughed. "I knew you wouldn't spend the whole night in that chair," he told her. "I just wanted to see how long it would take you to give up."

"Well, just because I did doesn't mean you should get any ideas," she growled.

"About what?" he asked, feigning innocence.

"You know what I'm talking about."

"Never crossed my mind."

"I'll bet."

"I'm serious," he insisted. "I'm used to it."

She wasn't sure she understood. "Used to what?"

"Doing without. I've been celibate for months."

She laughed. "Right," she said. "And I'm the Easter Bunny."

"I have!" He sounded properly insulted.

"You forget who you're talking to. I know you. You couldn't be celibate if your life depended on it!"

"That was the old me. This is the new me," he maintained.

"There's a difference?"

"You bet. And if you'd give me a chance, you'd find out I'm telling the truth."

"Give you a chance—"

"All in the world I've wanted since I came back from Dallas has been to try to make it work with you," he told her then. "It took a brush with death to make me realize how I really felt about you. That's what I was trying to tell you that day in the restaurant, but you weren't having any of it."

"What *I* was trying to tell *you* that day—but you weren't having any of it, either—was that I was willing to give it a shot, too, but that I wasn't willing to rush into anything. I wanted to take it slowly. One day at a time."

"Why didn't you tell me that?"

"You didn't give me a chance. You took off out of there before I could get the words out," she reminded him.

There was a long pause. "Well, I'm still willing if you are," he said finally.

She couldn't mask her surprise. "After all these years, after all that's gone wrong between us?" she asked.

"After all that," he assured her.

"Think we'd have a chance?" she wondered aloud.

"Sure. Why not?"

"Consider our track record."

"Okay, so we've been fighting like Yankees and Confederates since our second anniversary. Doesn't that tell you something?"

"Sure. It tells me we're incompatible."

"Nah. It tells me the old chemistry's still there," he said. "We wouldn't still be able to get to each other if we didn't still care so much."

"Nice theory."

"Not theory. Fact."

"Uh-huh."

"I'm serious."

"You couldn't be serious of your life depended on it."

"Sure I can. It's just easier this way," he told her. "You know the saying—I'm laughing to keep from crying."

She was silent for a moment. "Who made you cry, Mel?" she asked finally.

He drew in a deep breath. "It's a long story."

"I've got all night," she told him.

"Some other time, okay?"

"This isn't getting us off to a very good start, Mel," she pointed out.

He moved closer, kissing her gently. "One day at a time—just like you said," he whispered.

He wasn't ready to talk about *that*. Not yet.

Eleven

Eleven

By morning the rain had stopped.

Kathleen woke first, her sleep rudely interrupted by the bright morning sunlight streaming through the window. Removing Mel's arm from around her waist, where it had been for most of the night, she sat up on the edge of the bed and let out an exaggerated yawn. She hadn't slept so soundly in—well, a heck of a long time.

She hadn't slept with her ex-husband in a heck of a long time, either.

She smiled to herself. There had been a time she would rather have died than admit it, but she'd enjoyed it. She'd enjoyed sleeping with him even if sleeping was all they'd done together last night. Especially since that was all they'd done together. She'd never wanted sex to be the only bond between them. She'd never try to reconcile with him if all they had going for them was a strong physical attraction.

Last night, they'd just talked.

Do we have a chance? she wondered as she took her clothes and went into the bathroom to dress. Is is possible? Do I dare to hope?

She looked long and hard at her reflection in the small mirror over the sink, and she wished she'd brought her bag into the bathroom with her so she could have put on her makeup. Look at that face, she thought. You look like you slept in it.

The face looking back at her from the mirror made her willing to retrieve the bag. As she emerged from the bathroom, Mel, now awake and sitting upright, grinned. "Don't tell me you got dressed in the bathroom."

"And what if I did?" She picked up her bag.

"Jeez, Kathy, I've seen you—in a lot less," he reminded her. "We *were* married."

"That was then. This is now," she maintained.

He laughed. "What a deep, philosophical observation!"

"You know perfectly well what I'm talking about," she told him in a half-scolding tone.

He threw up his hands in mock exasperation. "Okay, okay—have it your way," he surrendered. "I'll observe the hands-off policy—for now, anyway."

"Look at it this way," she began. "If we can have a relationship without sex, then we've got a good shot at making this work."

"As brother and sister, maybe."

"Melvin—"

"Don't call me Melvin!"

She took the bag into the bathroom. He was saying something, but she couldn't hear him over the water running as she washed her face. Turning off the water, she reached for a towel.

"What did you say?" she called out to him as she patted her face gently with the towel.

"I said we could find a restaurant in town and have breakfast before we hit the road," he shouted back at her.

"Sounds good to me."

"I don't know about you, but I'm starving. Celibacy always makes me ravenous."

"Melvin!"

"Don't call me Melvin!"

He advanced on her menacingly. She backed off, laughing. "Now, Melvin—" she managed, choking on her own laughter.

"I told you not to call me Melvin!" In one sudden, swift movement, he grabbed her and threw her down on the bed. Straddling her, he pinned her arms at her sides. They were both laughing so hard they began to shake violently.

"C'mon, Mel—let me up!" she ordered unconvincingly.

"No way!" His grin was almost evil. "It would seem I have you in an—er—compromising position."

"And just *what* do you mean by that?" she wanted to know.

"Well, it would be easy—sooo easy—to take unfair advantage of you at the moment," he pointed out.

"You wouldn't!" she gasped.

"I might," he warned.

"We agreed—"

"Wrongo. *You* agreed. I don't recall having a voice in that decision."

"Baloney!"

He bent down to kiss her, and it was surprisingly tender. "Celibacy never did agree with me," he growled in her ear.

"Yes, I remember that about you." As he freed one of her arms to unbutton her blouse, she raised it to stop him, but he pushed it away.

"Not this time," he said firmly. "Anyway, I don't believe you really *want* me to stop at all."

"Oh, you don't, don't you?" She put up a half-hearted struggle but was thwarted by her own uncontrollable laughter.

"As *I* recall, celibacy never did sit too well with *you,* either," he said as he pushed her blouse and bra away to expose her breasts. Then he lowered his head and kissed her again. This time he didn't stop with her lips. He kissed her face, her eyes, her forehead. He kissed her neck, moving slowly down over her collarbone, lower, lower, along the deep cleft between her breasts. He was halfway across the flat plane of her belly when she spoke up.

"This isn't fair, Melvin."

He looked up with a silly smile on his face. "What isn't fair?" he asked dumbly.

"You have me here in this—ah—compromising position, and you, well, you're still dressed," she pointed out.

"This?" he asked, looking down at his T-shirt and briefs. "You call *this* dressed?"

"It's more than I have on at the moment."

"Easily remedied, m'dear," he assured her, peeling off his shirt. Tossing it aside, he quickly followed with the briefs.

"Now, where were we?" he asked, looking down at her. "Ah, yes." Before she could stop him, he finished removing the clothing that remained on the lower half of her body.

Her initial reservations about resuming a physical relationship with him dissolved in the fierce current of their mutual desires. They kissed, touched and explored each other's bodies with the urgency of first-time lovers.

Mel's hands explored her nakedness, moving over her with all the tenderness and careful exploration of a blind man trying to find his way in the darkness. Fingers moving from her face, down her throat, over her shoulders, he lingered at her breasts, cupping one in each hand, pressing them together as he bent his head to nuzzle them, first one, then the other. He flicked his tongue across the hard nubs at their centers, building her desire with the skill of a virtuoso playing a finely tuned instrument to a thundering crescendo.

She grasped his shoulders, digging her fingernails into his flesh as his lips began a slow journey upward again. "Why are you stopping?" she asked, suddenly alarmed.

"Not stopping. Just a moment to take necessary precautions."

"Necessary—" Then she saw the small piece of cellophane he was taking from the pocket of his discarded pants, which had been lying on the floor next to the bed. Of course. A condom.

"Prepared for all possible emergencies?" she asked with just a twinge of annoyance in her voice.

He gave her a puzzled look. "Now what's *that* for?"

"If you're carrying them around with you, you must have been expecting something to happen...with someone...." She always knew there had been other women since the divorce, but it was a whole new ballgame to be face-to-face with the evidence. She hadn't expected to feel so strongly about it.

"Let's just say I was hopeful." He opened it carefully.

"Anyone in particular in mind?" she asked icily.

"Oh, come on, Kathy!" he snorted. "I was hoping to—uh—"

"Get lucky?"

Now he was mad. "I was hoping—as I've been hoping for weeks now, for your information—that something might develop between you and me!"

"And you made a trip to the drugstore in my honor," she concluded somewhat sarcastically.

"Kathy, look, if you can't trust me—"

"I want to, but you don't make it easy."

"Did you expect me to be a monk all those years we were apart?" he wanted to know.

"Hardly," she said frostily. "I knew you too well for that."

"Are you telling me you never..."

"No, I didn't."

His eyes rolled skyward. "It figures!"

"What's *that* supposed to mean?"

"Kathy, you've got to be one of medical science's great unsolved mysteries," he told her, tossing the half-opened condom onto the nightstand. "You never—there was nobody in all those years? Seriously?"

"Scout's honor."

"Yeah—you would."

"Would what?"

"Be a scout."

"What kind of crack is that?"

He leaned forward, his eyes meeting hers. "There really wasn't anyone for you in all that time?"

"No one I cared enough about to make love with," she said. Alarms were going off in her head.

Why are you doing this? Are you deliberately try-ing to sabotage the reconciliation?

"I can't believe it."

"Are you making fun of me?" she demanded angrily.

"No...not at all." He shook his head emphati-cally. "I'm...touched."

She gave him a quizzical look.

"All those years...there was never anybody else for you."

"I guess I still loved you. Fool that I was."

"I was the fool."

She looked at him, not sure she'd heard cor-rectly. "What?"

"I was a fool. In spite of everything, you loved me. You did love me."

"I've always loved you, Mel."

He bent down to kiss her again, and this time he didn't stop. Nor did she try to stop him. She gave herself up to his kisses and caresses, clinging to him as he explored her once again with his hands and his mouth. When his fingers found their way to the core of her womanhood, she was ready for him. And when he started to put the condom on this time, she was more than happy to help him. In fact, it was the sexiest experience they'd ever shared...their hands together, joined in a task that was more sensual than she could have ever imagined, touching, stroking, kissing as they completed the job at hand. Then he lowered her to the bed again, still kissing her hungrily as he covered her body with his own and they were molded together in the heat of passion. She was swept away by her own overpowering desires as he took her, his lovemaking more intense and yet more tender than she remembered it ever being before. When it was over, they lay in each other's arms, kissing and whispering endearments.

"Mel?" Kathleen spoke his name softly. "I hate to ruin this beautiful moment between us, but—" She hesitated.

"Yeah?"

"I'm hungry."

There was only one restaurant in town, and it definitely wasn't a four-star establishment. It was a greasy-spoon-type diner where everything on the menu was cooked in enough oil to qualify the place for membership in OPEC, where the waitresses were surly and the customers even surlier.

"This place should have a warning from the surgeon general posted in the window," Kathleen complained, but only to Mel. "It's got to be the cholesterol equivalent of Chernobyl."

"This is a small town, sweetheart," he reminded her. "I doubt a health food operation would get much business here."

From their booth by the window, Kathleen watched the locals on the street in front of the restaurant. "You're probably right," she conceded.

"Look, there's something we need to talk about, kiddo," Mel said then, reaching across the table to take her hand in his. "If we're going to try to make a go of it—"

"Make a go of it?" Kathleen stifled a giggle.

"I'm serious," he insisted.

She pressed her fingers to her lips. "I'm sorry."

"This situation could present problems—the two books, I mean," he reminded her—as if she needed to be reminded. "It sure hasn't been easy up to now, and we haven't been involved."

Kathleen smiled knowingly. "I think we've always been *involved*," she disagreed. "We just didn't know it—or want to admit it, I'm not sure which. That's *why* it's been such a problem for us."

"Maybe." He didn't sound totally convinced. "Anyway, until these books are behind us, they're going to go on being a source of trouble for us."

"You're probably right," she said with a nod.

"Think we can keep our egos under control?"

"I can if you can," she said confidently.

"Easy to say now," he maintained, "but what about when the books are both out and we're waiting to see which one sells best? What about publicity?"

"I know it's not going to be easy," she said quietly, "but I get the feeling you're getting cold feet."

"Me?" He looked incredulous. "No way!"

"Then why do you keep bringing up all of the things that could go wrong?" she wanted to know.

"Because we have to face reality." He looked and sounded more serious than she remembered his ever being in all the years she'd known him. "If the two of us both being reporters was a problem for us before, what effect do you think this will have?"

Her eyes met his. "It was a problem for you, not me," she said.

He hesitated momentarily. "Okay—it was a problem for me," he said finally.

She smiled. "This is the first time you've openly admitted it," she told him.

"Yeah. So what?" Avoiding her eyes, he raked a hand through his hair nervously.

"I always had the feeling you had a problem with career women in general," she started, trying to ease her way into a conversation she knew wasn't going to be easy for either of them.

"No, I—" He stopped, changing his mind abruptly. "Yeah. Yeah, I guess I did."

"Why?" There was no delicate way to ask.

"I could say I'm just an old-fashioned kind of guy who thinks a woman's place is in the home," he suggested.

"You could," she agreed with a nod, "but I wouldn't believe you."

"You wouldn't, huh?"

She shook her head. "Nope."

"It's a long story."

"You said that before. I'm not letting you off the hook this time."

He was silent for a moment, looking down at his plate. "You know the old story about shrinks blaming all of a guy's problems on his mother?" he asked finally.

She nodded.

He frowned. "Well, in my case it's true."

She studied him intently. "You know, in all the years I've known you, I can't remember you mentioning your mother more than once or twice," she recalled.

Mel shrugged. "I never knew enough about her to say more," he admitted.

Kathleen said nothing, waiting for him to go on.

"My mother walked out on me and my dad when I was a kid. I was barely old enough to remember anything—but I remember that. A lot more clearly than I'd like."

"Why did she leave?" Kathleen asked, fairly certain his mother had been an ambitious woman but hoping there might have been more to it than just a woman choosing to pursue a career. Like marital problems, she thought. Like basic incompatibility.

"Because she wanted a career more than she wanted a family," he said, his voice full of contempt. "Because a husband and son just didn't fit into her plans."

"I'm sorry," she said softly.

He wouldn't look at her. "I cried myself to sleep every night for two years after that," he remembered. "By the end of that time, I'd come to hate her so much that I couldn't cry. I couldn't feel anything for her but contempt."

"What about your father?" she asked carefully.

"Oh, he was hurting, too," Mel said, "but he tried hard not to show it. He'd loved her. He had a hard time accepting the fact that a *job* meant more to her than we did. I don't think he ever stopped believing that one day she'd come back. He died believing it."

"But you didn't," Kathleen concluded.

He shook his head. "I did at first—or at least I *wished* she'd come back," he admitted. "After a while, I wished she was dead."

"But you didn't mean it."

"Oh, yes, I did," he insisted, picking at the tableware nervously. "I hated her for what she'd done to us. I wanted her to be punished for it."

"She never came back? Not at all?"

"Nope. Never even wrote—not so much as a postcard in all those years." He paused. "I remember when I was ten years old, spending the weekend with a friend. He had a wonderful mother—she took us places, spent time with us, she was there. She was just *there,* and that's the way it should be. She adored her kid and it showed. And I remember being so jealous I couldn't stand it."

She was silent for a long moment. "It must have been awful for you," she said finally.

He shrugged. "I got over it."

"Did you?"

He gave her a quizzical look.

"Seems you've still got a pretty low opinion of ambitious women," she pointed out.

His jaw tightened visibly. "Maybe—"

"No maybe about it."

"You didn't let me finish," he said crossly. "I was going to say maybe I just don't want to get burned again."

"Not all of us are alike, you know," she told him.

"No? You walked out."

"I couldn't accept the idea of having to give up something I'd worked so hard for," she responded honestly. "I wanted a career."

"I rest my case," he said with a twinge of sarcasm in his voice.

"I wanted my career," she repeated, "but I also wanted you. I wanted our marriage—and, eventually, I wanted children. I love you, Mel. I would never have left you if you hadn't made it impossible for me to stay."

His eyes met hers. "I don't know if my feelings will ever change," he confessed.

She smiled. "I'm willing to take my chances."

Mel was having second thoughts.

Well, not second thoughts, really, but doubts. Definitely doubts. Doubts he couldn't, *wouldn't* share with Kathy. Not now. Not yet. But the doubts were there, and they had to be dealt with.

He'd told her that he wanted a future with her. But he'd been honest about his feelings. He'd told her he didn't know if his feelings about ambitious women would ever change, and he didn't. The scars his mother had inflicted upon him weren't going to just disappear overnight.

You've got to be a ten-plus on the idiot scale, Riggs! he told himself. This is not your mother. This is Kathy—and you've been moving heaven and earth to get her back for months now. Are you going to be a fool and blow it?

But he couldn't help himself. In his mind, he saw a small boy crying for his unfeeling mother as she climbed into a taxi and left without so much as a backward glance...Kathleen packing her bags that morning in Michigan after he'd insisted on coming back to their place, telling him she wanted a divorce...why? Why did it have to be that way?

He told himself Kathy wasn't like his mother. He reminded himself repeatedly of how much he loved her and needed her. How much he wanted to be married to her again.

All those years... there was never anybody else for you.

I guess I still loved you. Fool that I was.

I was the fool. In spite of everything, you loved me. You did love me.

"She did love me," he said aloud, suddenly glad he was alone for the moment. If anyone had heard him, they would have thought he was crazy.

"She *does* love me."

She's not my mother, he kept telling himself. She's not going to run out on me just because my mother did.

She left once before.

But I drove her away.

I'll drive her away again if I don't stop thinking like this.

So what am I more afraid of? Getting hurt or losing Kathy for good?

He couldn't lose her. Coming to terms with his feelings and fear was a chance he was simply going to have to take.

"You know, we're probably doing all of this for nothing," Mel said. "They'll end up declaring a mistrial, and both of our contacts will be cancelled."

"You seem awfully sure about that." Kathleen studied the crude map drawn for them by the old man at the service station where they'd stopped for gas.

"I've seen it happen before."

She looked at him. "I never knew you did time as a court reporter."

"Oh, yeah—when I first came to Saint Louis," he recalled. "I started out in traffic court—talk about boring!"

"I'm just beginning to realize just how much about you I don't know," she said.

"We've been apart a lot of years," he reminded her.

"Yeah." And after a long pause: "Why didn't you ever tell me about your mother before?"

He kept his eyes on the road. "It wasn't something I wanted—or even could—talk about," he said quietly.

"You're talking about it now."

"It's taken time," he said. "Time and the realization that you and I had no chance of making it this time around unless I did open up about it."

"I'm glad you did."

"So am I."

The road was worse than bad. It wasn't even paved, just a narrow gravel road—and not even much of that. There were a lot of deep ruts that, since last night's rain, were filled with water. It's a miracle we haven't gotten stuck, Kathleen thought. So far, anyway.

The farther they traveled, the more relieved she was that she'd left her car in town and come with Mel.

For more reasons than one.

"Oh, no—just what we don't need!" Mel snorted.

Her head jerked up. "What's wrong?"

"Look." He gestured toward the road in front of them. A roadblock had been set up, bearing an unmistakable message: Bridge Washed Out.

"Must've happened during the storm last night," Mel said, tapping his hand against the steering wheel impatiently.

"What do we do now?" Kathleen wondered aloud.

Mel took a deep breath. "Not much we can do."

"We're turning back?"

"For now, yeah." He put the car in reverse.

"There has to be another route."

"Maybe, maybe not."

"There has to be another route," she repeated insistently. "People living on the other side have to be able to get to town."

"Not if the bridge is out. Besides, there *are* other towns," he said, "over there."

She nodded once. "Right."

He muttered an oath as the car jerked to a stop.

"What's wrong?" Kathleen asked. The wheels were spinning, but the car wasn't moving.

"I'd say we're stuck." He was more than a little annoyed as he got out of the car. "Get behind the wheel. When I tell you to, give it gas."

She nodded and climbed into his seat, realizing at that moment that she didn't really like bucket seats at all.

Watching the rearview mirror, she saw him take a shovel from the trunk. He's always prepared for everything, she thought, amused.

By the time he finished, there was more mud on his clothes than there was on the road—or that was how it looked to Kathleen, anyway.

"Now!" he called out to her.

"Aye, aye, captain!" she responded, saluting smartly. Depressing the accelerator, she looked up at the rearview mirror. Mud was flying in every direction—but at least the car was moving.

"Stop!" he yelled, waving.

"We're out?" she asked as he threw the shovel back in the trunk and brought a plastic leaf bag forward to sit on and protect his seat.

"We're out. Now I need a nice hot shower."

She laughed, returning to her own seat. "A textbook understatement if I ever heard one."

"How would you feel about calling it a day?" he asked. "I'm beat. We can take another shot at it in the morning."

She looked at him, trying to laugh. "I don't think we really have a choice."

At that moment, the voice of a newscaster on the car radio caught their attention. "The Henry Rollins trial ended this morning when a mistrial was declared...Mr. Rollins, a prominent Dallas businessman accused of murdering his wife..."

Mel started to laugh hysterically. Kathleen thought he *was* hysterical. "Mel—" she began, worried.

"This is great! This is really great!"

"Great?" Now she was really confused.

"Sure. All the things we worried about—they aren't problems anymore," he pointed out.

"You don't mind having your contract canceled?" she asked.

"There'll be other books," he said confidently. "Actually, I'll be glad to be rid of Washburn. I never was crazy about working with that jerk."

"I can imagine."

"What about you?"

"I'm disappointed," she admitted. "That contract meant a lot to me."

"As I recall, you always wanted to write fiction," he remembered.

"Well—yes."

"Maybe now is the time to take a shot at a novel," he suggested.

She looked at him warily. "How would you feel about that?" she wanted to know.

He grinned. "Ask me after it sells," he told her.

"Mel—" she began.

"We've both got a lot to work out," he said, resting a muddy hand on her knee, "but we're older and—I hope—wiser than we were the first time around."

"You really think so?"

"Well," he said with a wink, "the Berlin Wall *did* come down."

She laughed. "Nut! As long as we no longer have a reason to stick around here, why don't we go home?"

He smiled. "Home?"

He liked the sound of that.

Epilogue

Six months later

"This gets worse every year," Mel complained as he navigated his car through the heavy traffic—automobile and pedestrian—downtown. He and Kathleen, who'd left the *Mirror* four months ago to join the *Star* staff, were now living together and blissfully ignoring Rollins's new trial. Today they were doing something they hadn't done in a long time: taking a day off to enjoy the sights and sounds of the VP Fair, the annual Fourth of July festival held on the Saint Louis riverfront.

"You have all kinds of trouble getting through the traffic, and when you finally *do*, you can't find a place to park. The food's overpriced, the weather's always either too hot or it rains every day of the festivities, and every year, somebody gets shot, stabbed or robbed."

"So why do you insist on going?" Kathleen asked, trying not to laugh. She already knew the answer. He was like a kid when the circus came to town. He loved it.

"One of these days I'll get enough and decide to stay home," he was saying.

"Right."

"I think I saw a parking place back there." He promptly made an illegal U-turn.

"Still the maverick, aren't you?" she asked, bracing herself with both hands on the dashboard.

He chuckled. "What can I say? Some habits are just too hard to break."

"Not all of them, I hope."

He looked at her suspiciously out of the corner of his eye. "Why do I get the feeling this is all leading somewhere?" he wanted to know.

She promptly confessed. "I was just wondering...when are you going to marry me?"

He hit the brakes, bringing the already slow-moving traffic to an abrupt halt and nearly causing a multicar collision. "You wanna run that past me again?" he asked, not sure he'd heard correctly.

"I said, when are you going to marry me?" she repeated emphatically.

He hooted with laughter. "Is that a proposal?"

"Well," she began with a totally serious look on her face, "I figure one of us has to pop the question, and it sure didn't look like you were ever going to do it."

"I thought you were the one who wanted to take things one day at a time—"

"One *day* at a time, Riggs. Not one *year* at a time."

"Let me get this straight," he started.

"Quit nitpicking," she said with mock anger in her voice. "Are you going to marry me or not?"

"This is all so sudden—"

"Melvin!"

"Don't call me Melvin!"

"This is the last time I'm going to ask," she warned him.

"It's not much of a proposal," he observed.

"It's the only one you're going to get," she shot back at him.

"No bended knee?"

"No bended knee."

"I don't know...."

"Last chance, Riggs."

"Well, when you put it that way—yes."

"When?"

"Today," he decided promptly.

"Be serious!"

"I *am* serious."

"There's no way—"

"Sure there is. We get married today—right here, right now, or not at all."

"And just *how* do you suggest we do it?" she wanted to know.

"City Hall's right up the street," he said with an offhanded gesture. "We can get the license and do it right there at that little mobile marriage chapel on their parking lot."

She made a face. "The one with the ugly purple curtains in the back window?" she asked.

He nodded. "That's the one."

"I was thinking of something a little more—romantic," she admitted.

"And me in one of those monkey suits?" he asked. "No way, honey!"

Kathleen drew in a deep breath. "How, pray tell, are we ever going to make a go of marriage when we can't even agree on the wedding?"

"It's now or never," he pressured her.

"But it's so—tacky!"

"It's not the surroundings, but the two people involved that counts—isn't that what you've always told me?"

"We're not exactly dressed for a wedding—even an informal one—"

"So we'll have the most unique wedding photo in town. It suits us, don't you think?"

"I'm not sure how to take that."

"We'll need a ring," he said thoughtfully.

"There's a jeweler over on Ninth and Locust," she offered.

"The drugstore's closer."

"Drugstore?"

"We still have perfectly good rings from the first time around," he reminded her. "You *do* still have your ring, don't you?"

"I think so." As if she would ever have parted with it!

"So we sure don't need new ones. I'll just get one out of the gum machine to get us through the ceremony—"

"Gum machine?"

"You've got a better idea?"

She took a deep breath, admitting—but only to herself—that it was entirely appropriate. It was also appropriate that they should marry now, during the Fourth of July celebration.

After all, they could spend their wedding night watching the fireworks show. Or maybe they'd just do one of their own.

*   *   *   *   *

NORA ROBERTS

Love has a language all its own, and for centuries, flowers have symbolized love's finest expression. Discover the language of flowers—and love—in this romantic collection of 48 favorite books by bestselling author Nora Roberts.

Starting in February 1992, two titles will be available each month at your favorite retail outlet.

In February, look for:

Irish Thoroughbred, Volume #1
The Law Is A Lady, Volume #2

Collect all 48 titles and become fluent in the Language of Love.

LOL192

THE LANGUAGE of LOVE

Silhouette Special Edition®

salutes

MOMENTS OF GLORY

from Lindsay McKenna

In a country torn with conflict, in a time of bitter passions, these brave men and women wage a war against all odds . . . and a timeless battle for honor, for fleeting moments of glory, for the promise of enduring love.

February: RIDE THE TIGER (#721) Survivor Dany Villard is wise to the love-'em-and-leave-'em ways of war, but wounded hero Gib Ramsey swears she's captured his heart . . . forever.

March: ONE MAN'S WAR (#727) The war raging inside brash and bold Captain Pete Mallory threatens to destroy him, until Tess Ramsey's tender love guides him toward peace.

April: OFF LIMITS (#733) Soft-spoken Marine Jim McKenzie saved Alexandra Vance's life in Vietnam; now he needs her love to save his honor. . . .

YOU'VE ASKED FOR IT, YOU'VE GOT IT!

MAN OF THE MONTH: 1992

ONLY FROM

SILHOUETTE® *Desire*™

You just couldn't get enough of them, those sexy men from Silhouette Desire—twelve sinfully sexy, delightfully devilish heroes. Some will make you sweat, some will make you sigh . . . but every long, lean one of them will have you swooning. So here they are, men we couldn't resist bringing to you for one more year. . . .

A KNIGHT IN TARNISHED ARMOR
by Ann Major in January

THE BLACK SHEEP
by Laura Leone in February

THE CASE OF THE MESMERIZING BOSS
by Diana Palmer in March

DREAM MENDER
by Sheryl Woods in April

WHERE THERE IS LOVE
by Annette Broadrick in May

BEST MAN FOR THE JOB
by Dixie Browning in June

Don't let these men get away! *Man of the Month*, only in Silhouette Desire.